IM_AGIN_E

Ghosts, gods, and devils—
    Heavens and hells—
      Cities in the sky and cities in the sea.

Now try time machines and space ships.
    Certainly you can imagine Martians, but
    how about inter-planetary vampires?
        Or a mouse that isn't a mouse?

Fred Brown says anyone can imagine
    these things.
      (Like riding a seal, we'd say.)
But **HONEYMOON IN HELL** proves that
      Brown can imagine things we
couldn't even begin to imagine imagining.

Books by Fredric Brown

- THE LENIENT BEAST
- THE DEAD RINGER
- THE FABULOUS CLIPJOINT
- HIS NAME WAS DEATH
- NIGHT OF THE JABBERWOCK
- DEATH HAS MANY DOORS
- THE FAR CRY
- THE WENCH IS DEAD
- WHAT MAD UNIVERSE
- THE LIGHTS IN THE SKY ARE STARS
- STAR SHINE (ANGELS AND SPACESHIPS)
- MARTIANS, GO HOME
- SCIENCE FICTION CARNIVAL
- SPACE ON MY HANDS
- ROGUE IN SPACE
- THE SCREAMING MIMI

- Published by Bantam Books

FREDRIC BROWN

HONEYMOON IN HELL

Bantam Books, Inc.

HONEYMOON IN HELL

A Bantam Book / published August 1958

COPYRIGHT NOTICES AND ACKNOWLEDGMENTS

HONEYMOON IN HELL reprinted from Galaxy Science Fiction by permission of World Editions Inc. Copyright, 1950, by World Editions Inc.

TOO FAR reprinted from the Magazine of Fantasy and Science Fiction by permission of Fantasy House, Inc. Copyright, 1955, by Fantasy House, Inc.

MAN OF DISTINCTION reprinted from Thrilling Wonder Stories by permission of Standard Magazines, Inc. Copyright, 1950, by Standard Magazines, Inc.

MILLENNIUM reprinted from the Magazine of Fantasy and Science Fiction by permission of Fantasy House, Inc. Copyright, 1955, by Fantasy House, Inc.

THE DOME reprinted from Thrilling Wonder Stories by permission of Standard Magazines, Inc. Copyright, 1951, by Standard Magazines, Inc.

BLOOD reprinted from the Magazine of Fantasy and Science Fiction by permission of Fantasy House, Inc. Copyright, 1954, by Fantasy House, Inc.

HALL OF MIRRORS reprinted from Galaxy Science Fiction by permission of Galaxy Publishing Corp. Copyright, 1953, by Galaxy Publishing Corp.

EXPERIMENT reprinted from Galaxy Science Fiction by permission of Galaxy Publishing Corp. Copyright, 1954, by Galaxy Publishing Corp.

THE LAST MARTIAN reprinted from Galaxy Science Fiction by permission of World Editions Inc. Copyright, 1950, by World Editions Inc.

SENTRY reprinted from Galaxy Science Fiction by permission of Galaxy Publishing Corp. Copyright, 1954, by Galaxy Publishing Corp.

MOUSE reprinted from Thrilling Wonder Stories by permission of Standard Magazines, Inc. Copyright, 1949, by Standard Magazines, Inc.

NATURALLY reprinted from Beyond by permission of Galaxy Publishing Corp. Copyright, 1954, by Galaxy Publishing Corp.

"ARENA" reprinted from Astounding Science Fiction by permission of Street & Smith Publications, Inc. Copyright, 1944, by Street & Smith Publications, Inc.

VOODOO reprinted from Beyond by permission of Galaxy Publishing Corp. Copyright, 1954, by Galaxy Publishing Corp.

KEEP OUT reprinted from Amazing Stories by permission of Ziff-Davis Publishing Co. Copyright, 1953, by Ziff-Davis Publishing Co.

FIRST TIME MACHINE reprinted from Ellery Queen's Mystery Magazine by permission of Mercury Publications, Inc. Copyright, 1955, by Mercury Publications, Inc.

AND THE GODS LAUGHED reprinted from Planet Stories by permission of Love Romances Publishing Co., Inc. Copyright, 1943, by Love Romances Publishing Co., Inc.

THE WEAPON reprinted from Astounding Science Fiction by permission of Street & Smith Publications, Inc. Copyright, 1951, by Street & Smith Publications, Inc.

A WORD FROM OUR SPONSOR reprinted from Other Worlds by permission of Clark Publishing Co. Copyright, 1951, by Clark Publishing Co.

RUSTLE OF WINGS reprinted from the Magazine of Fantasy and Science Fiction by permission of Fantasy House, Inc. Copyright, 1953, by Fantasy House, Inc.

IMAGINE reprinted from the Magazine of Fantasy and Science Fiction by permission of Fantasy House, Inc. Copyright, 1955, by Fantasy House, Inc.

Bantam Books are published by Bantam Books, Inc. Its trade-mark, consisting of the words "Bantam Books" and the portrayal of a bantam, is registered in the U. S. Patent Office and in other countries. Marca Registrada. Printed in the United States of America. Bantam Books, Inc., 25 W. 45th St., New York 36, N. Y.

CONTENTS

HONEYMOON IN HELL

ON SEPTEMBER 16th in the year 1962, things were going along about the same as usual, only a little worse. The cold war that had been waxing and waning between the United States and the Eastern Alliance—Russia, China, and their lesser satellites—was warmer than it had ever been. War, hot war, seemed not only inevitable but extremely imminent.

The race for the Moon was an immediate cause. Each nation had landed a few men on it and each claimed it. Each had found that rockets sent from Earth were inadequate to permit establishment of a permanent base upon the Moon, and that only establishment of a permanent base, in force, would determine possession. And so each nation (for convenience we'll call the Eastern Alliance a nation, although it was not exactly that) was engaged in rushing construction of a space station to be placed in an orbit around Earth.

With such an intermediate step in space, reaching the Moon with large rockets would be practicable and construction of armed bases, heavily garrisoned, would be comparatively simple. Whoever got there first could not only *claim* possession, but could implement the claim. Military secrecy on both sides kept from the public just how near to completion each space base was, but it was generally—and correctly—believed that the issue would be determined within a year, two years at the outside.

Neither nation could *afford* to let the other control the Moon. That much had become obvious even to those who were trying desperately to maintain peace.

On September 17th, 1962, a statistician in the birth

record department of New York City (his name was Wilbur Evans, but that doesn't matter) noticed that out of 813 births reported the previous day, 657 had been girls and only 156 boys.

He knew that, statistically, this was practically impossible. In a small city where there are only, say, ten births a day, it is quite possible—and not at all alarming—that on any one given day, 90% or even 100%, of the births may be of the same sex. But out of so large a figure as 813, so high a ratio as 657 to 156 *is* alarming.

Wilbur Evans went to his department chief and he, too, was interested and alarmed. Checks were made by telephone—first with nearby cities and, as the evidence mounted, with more and more distant ones.

By the end of that day, the puzzled investigators—and there was quite a large group interested by then—knew that in every city checked, the same thing had happened. The births, all over the Western Hemisphere and in Europe, for that day had averaged about the same—three boys for every thirteen girls.

Back-checking showed that the trend had started almost a week before, but with only a slight predominance of girls. For only a few days had the discrepancy been obvious. On the fifteenth, the ratio had been three boys to every five girls and on the sixteenth it had been four to fourteen.

The newspapers got the story, of course, and kicked it around. The television comics had fun with it, if their audiences didn't. But four days later, on September 21st, only one child out of every eighty-seven born in the country was male. That wasn't funny. People and governments started to worry; biologists and laboratories who had already started to investigate the phenomenon made it their number one project. The television comics quit joking about it after one crack on the subject by the top comedian in the country drew 875,480 indignant letters and lost him his contract.

On September 29th, out of a normal number of births in the United States, only forty-one were boys. Investigation proved that every one of these was a late, or delayed, birth. It became obvious that no male child had been conceived during the latter part of December of the previous year, 1961. By this time, of course, it was known that the same condition prevailed everywhere—in the countries of the Eastern Alliance as well as in the United States, and in every other country and area of the world—among the Eskimos, the Ubangi and the Indians of Tierra del Fuego.

The strange phenomenon, whatever it was, affected human beings only, however. Births among animals, wild or domesticated, showed the usual ratio of the two sexes.

Work on both space stations continued, but talk of war—and incidents tending to lead to war—diminished. The human race had something new, something less immediate, but in the long run far worse to worry about. Despite the apparent inevitability of war, few people thought that it would completely end the human race; a complete lack of male children definitely would. Very, very definitely.

And for once something was happening that the United States could not blame on the Eastern Alliance, and vice versa. The Orient—China and India in particular—suffered more, perhaps, than the Occident, for in those countries male offspring are of supreme emotional importance to parents. There were riots in both China and India, very bloody ones, until the people realized that they didn't know whom or what they were rioting against and sank back into miserable passivity.

In the more advanced countries, laboratories went on twenty-four-hour shifts, and anyone who knew a gene from a chromosome could command his weight in paper currency for looking—however futilely—through a microscope. Accredited biologists and geneticists became more important than presidents and dictators. But they accomplished no more than the cults which sprang up everywhere (though mostly in California) and which blamed what was happening on everything from a conspiracy of the Elders of Zion to (with unusually good sense) an invasion from space, and advocated everything from vegetarianism to (again with unusually good sense) a revival of phallic worship.

Despite scientists and cults, despite riots and resignation, not a single male child was born anywhere in the world during the month of December, 1962. There had been isolated instances, all quite late births, during October and November.

January of 1963 again drew a blank. Not that everyone qualified wasn't trying.

Except, perhaps, the one person who was slated to do more than anyone else—well, almost anyone else—about the matter.

Not that Capt. Raymond F. Carmody, U.S.S.F., retired, was a misogamist, exactly. He liked women well enough, both in the abstract and in the concrete. But he'd been badly jilted once and it had cured him of any desire whatsoever for marriage. Marriage aside, he took women as he found them—and he had no trouble finding them.

For one thing, don't let the word "retired" fool you. In the Space Service, rocket pilots are retired at the ripe old age of twenty-five. The recklessness, reaction-speed and stamina of youth are much more important than experience. The trick in riding a rocket is not to *do* anything in particular; it's to be tough enough to stay alive and sane until you get there. Technicians do the brain-work and the only controls are braking rockets to help you get down in one piece when you land; reaction-speed is of more importance than experience in managing them. Neither speed nor experience helps you if you've gone batty en route from spending days on end in the equivalent of a coffin, or if you haven't what it takes not to die in a good landing. And a good landing is one that you can walk away from after you've recovered consciousness.

That's why Ray Carmody, at twenty-seven, was a retired rocket pilot. Aside from test flights on and near Earth, he'd made one successful flight to the Moon with landing and return. It had been the fifteenth attempt and the third success. There had been two more successful flights thereafter—altogether five successful round trips out of eighteen tries.

But each rocket thus far designed had been able, barely, to carry fuel to get itself and its crew of one back to Earth, with almost-starvation rations for the period required. Step-rockets were needed to do even that, and step-rockets are terrifically expensive and cumbersome things.

At the time Carmody had retired from the Space Service, two years before, it had been conceded that establishment of a permanent base of any sort on the Moon was completely impracticable until a space station, orbited around the Earth, had been completed as a way-station. Comparatively huge rockets could reach a space station with relative ease, and starting *from* a station in open space and against lesser gravitational pull from Earth, going the rest of the way to the Moon would be even simpler.

But we're getting away from Ray Carmody, as Carmody had got away from the Space Service. He could have had a desk job in it after old age had retired him, a job that would have paid better than he was making at the moment. But he knew little about the technical end of rocketry, and he knew less, and cared nothing, about administrative detail work. He was most interested in cybernetics, which is the science of electronic calculating machines. The big machines had always fascinated him, and he'd found a job working with the biggest of them all, the one in the building on a corner of the grounds of the Pentagon that had been built, in 1958, especially to house it.

It was, of course, known as Junior to its intimates.

Carmody's job, specifically, was Operative, Grade I, and the Grade I meant that—despite his fame as one of the few men who had been to the Moon and lived to tell about it, and despite his ultra-honorable discharge with the grade of captain—his life had been checked back to its very beginning to be sure that he had not, even in his cradle, uttered a careless or subversive word.

There were only three other Grade I Operatives qualified to ask Junior questions and transmit his answers on questions which involved security—and that included questions on logistics, atomics, ballistics and rocketry, military plans of all sorts and everything else the military forces consider secret, which is practically everything except the currently preferred color of an infantryman's uniform.

The Eastern Alliance would undoubtedly have traded three puppet dictators and the tomb of Lenin to have had an agent, or even a sympathizer, as a Grade I Operative on Junior. But even the Grade II Operatives, who handled only problems dealing with non-classified matters, were checked for loyalty with extreme care. Possibly lest they might ask Junior a subversive question or feed a subversive idea into his electronic equivalent of a brain.

But be that as it may, on the afternoon of February 2, 1963, Ray Carmody was the Operative on duty in the control room. The only Operative, of course; dozens of technicians were required from time to time to service Junior and feed him, but only one Operative at a time fed data into him or asked him questions. So Carmody was alone in the soundproofed control room.

Doing nothing, however, at the moment. He'd just fed into Junior a complicated mess of data on molecular structure in the chromosome mechanism and had asked Junior—for the ten-thousandth time, at least—the sixty-four dollar question bearing on the survival of the human race: Why all children were now females and what could be done about it.

It had been quite a chunk of data, this time, and no doubt Junior would take quite a few minutes to digest it, add it to everything else he'd ever been told and synthesize the whole. No doubt in a few minutes he'd say, "Data insufficient." At least to this moment that had been his only answer to the sixty-four dollar question.

Carmody sat back and watched Junior's complicated bank of dials, switches and lights with a bored eye. And because the intake-mike was shut off and Junior couldn't hear what he was saying anyway, and because the control room was soundproofed so no one else could hear him, either, he spoke freely.

"Junior," he said, "I'm afraid you're a washout on this particular deal. We've fed you everything that every geneticist, every chemist, every biologist in this half of the world knows, and all you do is come up with that 'data insufficient' stuff. What do you want—blood?

"Oh, you're pretty good on some things. You're a whiz on orbits and rocket fuels, but you just can't understand *women*, can you? Well, I can't either; I'll give you that. And I've got to admit you've done the human race a good turn on one deal—atomics. You convinced us that if we completed and used H-bombs, *both* sides would lose the coming war. I mean *lose*. And we've got inside information that the other side got the same answer out of your brothers, the cybernetics machines over there, so they won't build or use them, either. Winning a war with H-bombs is about like winning a wrestling match with hand grenades; it's just as unhealthful for you as for your opponent. But we weren't talking about hand grenades. We were talking about women. Or I was. Listen, Junior—"

A light, not on Junior's panel but in the ceiling, flashed on and off, the signal for an incoming intercommunicator call. It would be from the Chief Operative, of course; no one else could connect—by intercommunicator or any other method—with this control room.

Carmody threw a switch.

"Busy, Carmody?"

"Not at the moment, Chief. Just fed Junior that stuff on molecular structure of genes and chromosomes. Waiting for him to tell me it's not enough data, but it'll take him a few minutes yet."

"Okay. You're off duty in fifteen minutes. Will you come to my office as soon as you're relieved? The President wants to talk to you."

Carmody said, "Goody. I'll put on my best pinafore."

He threw the switch again. Quickly, because a green light was flashing on Junior's panel.

He reconnected the intake- and output-mikes and said, "Well, Junior?"

"Data insufficient," said Junior's level mechanical voice.

Carmody sighed and noted the machine's answer on the report ending in a question which he had fed into the mike. He said, "Junior, I'm ashamed of you. All right, let's see if there's anything else I can ask and get an answer to in fifteen minutes."

He picked up a pile of several files from the table in front of him and leafed through them quickly. None contained fewer than three pages of data.

"Nope," he said, "not a thing here I can give you in fifteen minutes, and Bob will be here to relieve me then."

He sat back and relaxed. He wasn't ducking work; experience had proven that, although an AE7 cybernetics machine could accept verbal data in conformance with whatever vocabulary it had been given, and translate that data into mathematical symbols (as it translated the mathematical symbols of its answer back into words and mechanically spoke the words), it could not adapt itself to a change of voice within a given operation. It could, and did, adjust itself to understanding, as it were, Carmody's voice or the voice of Bob Dana who would shortly relieve him. But if Carmody started on a given problem, he'd have to finish it himself, or Bob would have to clear the board and start all over again. So there was no use starting something he wouldn't have time to finish.

He glanced through some of the reports and questions to kill time. The one dealing with the space station interested him most, but he found it too technical to understand.

"But you won't," he told Junior. "Pal, I've got to give that to you; when it comes to anything except women, you're really *good.*"

The switch was open, but since no question had been asked, of course Junior didn't answer.

Carmody put down the files and glowered at Junior. "Junior," he said, "that's your weakness all right, women. And you can't have genetics without women, can you?"

"No," Junior said.

"Well, you do know that much. But even I know it. Look, here's one that'll stump you. That blonde I met at the party last night. What about her?"

"The question," said Junior, "is inadequately worded; please clarify."

Carmody grinned. "You want me to get graphic, but I'll fool you. I'll just ask you this—should I see her again?"

"No," said Junior, mechanically but implacably.

Carmody's eyebrows went up. "The devil you say. And may I ask why, since you haven't met the lady, you say that?"

"Yes. You may ask why."

That was one trouble with Junior; he always answered the question you actually asked, not the one you implied.

"Why?" Carmody demanded, genuinely curious now as to what answer he was going to receive. "Specifically, why should I not again see the blonde I met last night?"

"Tonight," said Junior, "you will be busy. Before tomorrow night you will be married."

Carmody almost literally jumped out of his chair. The cybernetics machine had gone stark raving crazy. It *must* have. There was no more chance of his getting married tomorrow than there was of a kangaroo giving birth to a portable typewriter. And besides and beyond that, Junior never made predictions of the future—except, of course, on such things as orbits and statistical extrapolation of trends.

Carmody was still staring at Junior's impassive panel with utter disbelief and considerable consternation when the red light that was the equivalent of a doorbell flashed in the ceiling. His shift was up and Bob Dana had come to relieve him. There wasn't time to ask any further questions and, anyway, "Are you crazy?" was the only one he could think of at the moment.

Carmody didn't ask it. He didn't want to know.

Carmody switched off both mikes and stood gazing at Junior's impassive panel for a long time. He shook his head, went to the door and opened it.

Bob Dana breezed in and then stopped to look at Carmody. He said, "Something the matter, Ray? You look like you'd just seen a ghost, if I may coin a cliché."

Carmody shook his head. He wanted to think before he talked to anybody—and if he did decide to talk, it should be to Chief Operative Reeber and not to anyone else. He said, "Just I'm a little beat, Bob."

"Nothing special up?"

"Nope. Unless maybe I'm going to be fired. Reeber wants to see me on my way out." He grinned. "Says the President wants to talk to me."

Bob chuckled appreciatively. "If he's in a kidding mood, then your job's safe for one more day. Good luck."

The soundproof door closed and locked behind Carmody, and he nodded to the two armed guards who were posted on duty outside it. He tried to think things out carefully as he walked down the long stretch of corridor to the Chief Operative's office.

Had something gone wrong with Junior? If so, it was his duty to report the matter. But if he did, he'd get himself in trouble, too. An Operative wasn't supposed to ask private questions of the big cybernetics machine—even big, important questions. The fact that it had been a joking question would make it worse.

But Junior had either given him a joking answer—and it couldn't be that, because Junior didn't have a sense of humor—or else Junior had made a flat, unadulterated error. Two of them, in fact. Junior had said that Carmody would be busy tonight and—well, a wheel *could* come off his idea of spending a quiet evening reading. But the idea of his getting married tomorrow was utterly preposterous. There wasn't a woman on Earth he had the slightest intention of marrying. Oh, someday, maybe, when he'd had a little more fun out of life and felt a little more ready to settle down, he might feel differently. But it wouldn't be for years. Certainly not tomorrow, not even on a bet.

Junior *had* to be wrong, and if he was wrong it was a matter of importance, a matter far more important than Carmody's job.

So be honest and report? He made his decision just before he reached the door of Reeber's office. A reasonable compromise. He didn't *know* yet that Junior was wrong. Not to a point of mathematical certainty—just a billion to one odds against. So he'd wait until even that possibility was eliminated, until it was proven beyond all possible doubt that Junior was wrong. Then he'd report what he'd done and take the rap, if there was a rap. Maybe he'd just be fined and warned.

He opened the door and stepped in. Chief Operative Reeber stood up and, on the other side of the desk, a tall gray-haired man stood also. Reeber said, "Ray, I'd like you to meet the President of the United States. He came here to talk to you. Mr. President, Captain Ray Carmody."

And it *was* the President. Carmody gulped and tried to avoid looking as though he was doing a double take, which he was. Then President Saunderson smiled quietly and held out his hand. "Very glad to know you, Captain," he said, and Carmody was able to make the considerable understatement that he felt honored to meet the President.

Reeber told him to pull up a chair and he did so. The President looked at him gravely. "Captain Carmody, you have been chosen to—have the opportunity to volunteer for a mission of extreme importance. There is danger involved, but it is less than the danger of your trip to the Moon. You made the third—wasn't it?—out of the five successful trips made by United States pilots?"

Carmody nodded.

"This time the risk you will take is considerably less. There has been much technological advance in rocketry since you left the service two years ago. The odds against a successful round trip—even without the help of the space station, and I fear its completion is still two years distant—are much less. In fact, you will have odds of ten to one in your favor, as against approximately even odds at the time of your previous trip."

Carmody sat up straighter. "My *previous* trip! Then this volunteer mission is another flight to the Moon? Certainly, Mr. President, I'll gladly—"

President Saunderson held up a hand. "Wait, you haven't heard all of it. The flight to the Moon and return is the only part that involves physical danger, but it is the least important part. Captain, this mission is, possibly, of more importance to humanity than the first flight to the Moon, even than the first flight to the stars—if and when we ever make it—will be. What's at stake is the survival of the human race so that someday it *can* reach the stars. Your flight to the Moon will be an attempt to solve the problem which otherwise—"

He paused and wiped his forehead with a handkerchief.

"Perhaps you'd better explain, Mr. Reeber. You're more familiar with the exact way the problem was put to your machine, and its exact answers."

Reeber said, "Carmody, you know what the problem is. You know how much data has been fed into Junior on it. You know some of the questions we've asked him, and that we've been able to eliminate certain things. Such as—well, it's caused by no virus, no bacteria, nothing like that. It's not anything like an epidemic, because it struck the whole Earth at once, simultaneously. Even native inhabitants of islands that had no contact with civilization.

"We know also that whatever happens—whatever molecular change occurs—happens in the zygote after impregnation, very shortly after. We asked Junior whether an invisible *ray* of some sort could cause this. His answer was that it was possible. And in answer to a further question, he answered that this ray or force is possibly being used by—enemies of mankind."

"Insects? Animals? Martians?"

Reeber waved a hand impatiently. "Martians, maybe, if there *are* any Martians. We don't know that yet. But extra-terrestrials, most likely. Now Junior couldn't give us answers on this because, of course, we haven't the relevant data. It would be guesswork for him as well as for us —and Junior, being mechanical, can't guess. But here's a possibility:

"Suppose some extra-terrestrials *have* landed somewhere on Earth and have set up a station that broadcasts a ray that is causing the phenomenon of all children being girl-children. The ray is undetectable; at least thus far we haven't been able to detect it. They'd be killing off the human race and getting themselves a nice new planet to live on, without having to fire a shot, without taking any risk or losses themselves. True, they'll have to wait a while for us to die off, but maybe that doesn't mean anything to them. Maybe they've got all the time there is, and aren't in the slightest hurry."

Carmody nodded slowly. "It sounds fantastic, but I guess it's possible. I guess a fantastic situation like this *has* to have a fantastic explanation. But what do we do about it? How do we even prove it?"

Reeber said, "We fed the possibility into Junior as a working assumption—not as a fact—and asked him how we could check it. He came up with the suggestion that a married couple spend a honeymoon on the Moon—and see if circumstances are any different there."

"And you want me to pilot them there?"

"Not exactly, Ray. A little more than that—"

Carmody forgot that the President was there. He said, "Good God, you mean you want me to— Then Junior *wasn't* crazy, after all!"

Shamefacedly, then, he had to explain about the extra-curricular question he'd casually asked Junior and the answer he'd got to it.

Reeber laughed. "Guess we'll overlook your violation of Rule 17 this time, Ray. That is, if you accept the mission. Now here's the—"

"Wait," Carmody said. "I still want to know something. How did Junior know I was going to be picked out? And for that matter, why am I?"

"Junior was asked for the qualifications he'd recommend for the—ah—bridegroom. He recommended a rocket pilot who had already made the trip successfully, even though he was a year or two over the technical retirement age of twenty-five. He recommended that loyalty be considered as an important factor, and that the holding of a governmental position of great trust would answer that. He further recommended that the man be single."

"*Why* single? Look, there are four other pilots who've made that trip, and they're all loyal, regardless of what job they're holding now. I know them all personally. And all of them are married except me. Why not send a man who's already got a ball and chain?"

"For the simple reason, Ray, that the woman to be sent must be chosen with even more care. You know how tough a Moon landing is; only one woman in a hundred would live through it and still be able to—I mean, there's almost a negligible chance that the wife of any one of the other four pilots would be the best qualified woman who could possibly be found."

"Hmmm. Well, I suppose Junior's got something there. Anyway, I see now how he knew *I'd* be chosen. Those qualifications fit me exactly. But listen, do I have to *stay* married to whatever female is Amazonian enough to make the trip? There's a limit somewhere, isn't there?"

"Of course. You will be legally married before your departure, but upon your return a divorce will be granted without question if both—or either one—of you wish. The offspring of the union, if any, will be cared for. Whether male or female."

"Hey, that's right," Carmody said. "There's only an even chance of hitting the jackpot in any case."

"Other couples will be sent. The first trip is the most difficult and most important one. After that, a base will be established. Sooner or later we'll get our answer. We'll have it if even one male child is conceived on the Moon. Not that that will help us find the station that's sending the rays, or to detect or identify the rays, but we'll know what's wrong and can narrow our inquiry. I take it that you accept?"

Carmody sighed. "I guess so. But it seems a long way to go for—Say, who's the lucky girl?"

Reeber cleared his throat. "I think you'd better explain this part to him, Mr. President."

President Saunderson smiled as Carmody looked toward him. He said, "There is a more important reason, which Mr. Reeber skipped, why we could not choose a man who was already married, Captain. This is being done on an international basis, for very important diplomatic reasons. The experiment is for the benefit of humanity, not any nation or ideology. Your wife will be a Russian."

"A *Commie?* You're kidding me, Mr. President."

"I am not. Her name is Anna Borisovna. I have not met her, but I am informed that she is a very attractive girl. Her qualifications are quite similar to yours, except, of course, that she has not been to the Moon. No woman has. But she has been a pilot of experimental rockets on short-range flights. And she is a cybernetics technician working on the big machine at Moscow. She is twenty-four. And not, incidentally, an Amazon. As you know, rocket pilots aren't chosen for bulk. There is an added advantage in her being chosen. She speaks English."

"You mean I've got to talk to her, too?"

Carmody caught the look Reeber flashed at him and he winced.

The President continued: "You will be married to her tomorrow by a beam-televised ceremony. You blast off, both of you, tomorrow night—at different times, of course, since one of you will leave from here, the other from Russia. You will meet on the Moon."

"It's a large place, Mr. President."

"That is taken care of. Major Granham—you know him, I believe?" Carmody nodded. "He will supervise your takeoff and the sending of the supply rockets. You will fly tonight—a plane has been prepared for you—from the airport here to Suffolk Rocket Field. Major Granham will brief you and give you full instructions. Can you be at the airport by seven-thirty?"

Carmody thought and then nodded. It was five-thirty now and there'd be a lot of things for him to do and arrange in two hours, but he could make it if he tried. And hadn't Junior told him he was going to be busy this evening?

"Only one thing more," President Saunderson said. "This is strictly confidential, until and unless the mission is successful. We don't want to raise hopes, either here or in the Eastern Alliance, and then have them smashed." He smiled. "And if you and your wife have any quarrels on the Moon, we don't want them to lead to international repercussions. So please—try to get along." He held out his hand. "That's all, except thanks."

Carmody made the airport in time and the plane was waiting for him, complete with pilot. He had figured that he would have to fly it himself, but he realized that it was better this way; he could get a bit of rest before they reached Suffolk Field.

He got a little, but not much. The plane was a hot ship that got him there in less than an hour. A liaison officer was waiting for him and took him immediately to Major Granham's office.

Granham got down to brass tacks almost before Carmody could seat himself in the offered chair.

He said, "Here's the picture. Since you got out of the service, we've tremendously increased the accuracy of our rockets, manned or otherwise. They're so accurate that, with proper care, we can hit within a mile of any spot on the Moon that we aim at. We're picking Hell Crater—it's a small one, but we'll put you right in the middle of it. You won't have to worry about steering; you'll hit within a mile of the center without having to use your braking rockets for anything except braking."

"Hell Crater?" Carmody said. "There isn't any."

"Our Moon maps have forty-two thousand named craters. Do you know them all? This one, incidentally, was named after a Father Maximilian Hell, S. J., who was once director of the Vienna Observatory in old Austria."

Carmody grinned. "Now you're spoiling it. How come it was picked as a honeymoon spot, though? Just because of the name?"

"No. One of the three successful flights the Russians made happened to land and take off there. They found the footing better than anywhere else either of us has landed. Almost no dust; you won't have to slog through knee-deep pumice when you're gathering the supply rockets. Probably a more recently formed crater than any of the others we've happened to land in or explore."

"Fair enough. About the rocket I go in—what's the payload besides myself?"

"Not a thing but the food, water and oxygen you'll need en route, and your spacesuit. Not even fuel for your return, although you'll return in the same rocket you go in. Everything else, including return fuel, will be there waiting for you; it's on the way now. We fired ten supply rockets last night. Since you take off tomorrow night, they'll get there forty-eight hours before you do. So—"

"Wait a minute," Carmody said. "On my first trip I carried fifty pounds payload besides my return fuel. Is this a smaller type of rocket?"

"Yes, and a much better one. Not a step-rocket like you used before. Better fuel and more of it; you can accelerate longer and at fewer gravities, and you'll get there quicker. Forty-four hours as against almost four days before. Last time you took four and half Gs for seven minutes. This time you'll get by with three Gs and have twelve minutes' acceleration before you reach *Brennschluss*—cut loose from Earth's gravitation. Your first trip, you *had* to carry return fuel and a little payload because we didn't have the accuracy to shoot a supply rocket after you— or before you—and be sure it'd land within twenty miles. All clear? After we're through talking here I'll take you to the supply depot, show you the type of supply rocket we're using and how to open and unload it. I'll give you an inventory of the contents of each of the twelve of them we sent."

"And what if all of them don't get there?"

"At least eleven of them will. And everything's duplicated; if any one rocket goes astray, you'll still have everything you need—for two people. And the Russians are firing an equal number of supply rockets, so you'll have a double factor of safety." He grinned. "If none of our rockets get there, you'll have to eat borsht and drink vodka, maybe, but you won't starve."

"Are you kidding about the vodka?"

"Maybe not. We're including a case of Scotch, transferred to lightweight containers, of course. We figure it might be just the icebreaker you'll need for a happy honeymoon."

Carmody grunted.

"So maybe," Granham said, "the Russians'll figure the same way and send along some vodka. And the rocket fuels for your return, by the way, are not identical, but they're interchangeable. Each side is sending enough for the return of two rockets. If our fuel doesn't get there, you divvy with her, and vice versa."

"Fair enough. What else?"

"Your arrival will be just after dawn—Lunar time. There'll be a few hours when the temperature is somewhere between horribly cold and broiling hot. You'd better take advantage of them to get the bulk of your work done. Gathering supplies from the rockets and putting up the prefab shelter that's in them, in sections. We've got a duplicate of it in the supply depot and I want you to practice assembling it."

"Good idea. It's airtight and heatproof?"

"Airtight once you paint the seams with a special preparation that's included. And, yes, the insulation is excellent. Has a very ingenious little airlock on it, too. You won't have to waste oxygen getting in and out."

Carmody nodded. "Length of stay?" he asked.

"Twelve days. Earth days, of course. That'll give you plenty of time to get off before the Lunar night."

Granham chuckled. "Want instructions to cover those twelve days? No? Well, come on around to the depot then. I'll introduce you to your ship and show you the supply rockets and the shelter."

It turned out to be a busy evening, all right. Carmody didn't get to bed until nearly morning, his head so swimming with facts and figures that he'd forgotten it was his wedding day. Granham let him sleep until nine, then sent an orderly to wake him and to state that the ceremony had been set for ten o'clock and that he'd better hurry.

Carmody couldn't remember what "the ceremony" was for a moment, then he shuddered and hurried.

A Justice of the Peace was waiting for him there and technicians were working on a screen and projector. Granham said, "The Russians agreed that the ceremony could be performed at this end, provided we made it a civil ceremony. That's all right by you, isn't it?"

"It's lovely," Carmody told him. "Let's get on with it. Or don't we have to? As far as I'm concerned—"

"You know what the reaction of a lot of people would be when they learn about it, if it wasn't legal," Granham said. "So quit crabbing. Stand right there."

Carmody stood right there. A fuzzy picture on the beam-television screen was becoming clearer. And prettier. President Saunderson had not exaggerated when he'd said that Anna Borisovna was attractive and that she was definitely not an Amazon. She was small, dark, slender and very definitely attractive and not an Amazon.

Carmody felt glad that nobody had corned it up by putting her in a wedding costume. She wore the neat uniform of a technician, and she filled it admirably and curved it at the right places. Her eyes were big and dark and they were serious until she smiled at him. Only then did he realize that the connection was two-way and that she was seeing him.

Granham was standing beside him. He said, "Miss Borisovna, Captain Carmody."

Carmody said, inanely, "Pleased to meet you," and then redeemed it with a grin.

"Thank you, Captain." Her voice was musical and only faintly accented. "It is a pleasure."

Carmody began to think it would be, if they could just keep from arguing politics.

The Justice of the Peace stepped forward into range of the projector. "Are we ready?" he asked.

"A second," Carmody said. "It seems to me we've skipped a customary preliminary. Miss Borisovna, will you marry me?"

"Yes. And you may call me Anna."

She even has a sense of humor, Carmody thought, astonished. Somehow, he hadn't thought it possible for a Commie to have a sense of humor. He'd pictured them as all being dead serious about their ridiculous ideology and about everything else.

He smiled at her and said, "All right, Anna. And you may call me Ray. Are you ready?"

When she nodded, he stepped to one side to allow the Justice of the Peace to share the screen with him. The ceremony was brief and businesslike.

He couldn't, of course, kiss the bride or even shake

hands with her. But just before they shut off the projector, he managed to grin at her and say, "See you in Hell, Anna."

And he'd begun to feel certain that it wouldn't be that at all, really.

He had a busy afternoon going over every detail of operation of the new type rocket, until he knew it inside and out better than he did himself. He even found himself being briefed on details of the Russian rockets, both manned and supply types, and he was surprised (and inwardly a bit horrified) to discover to what extent the United States and Russia had been exchanging information and secrets. It couldn't all have happened in a day or so.

"How long has this been going on?" he demanded of Granham.

"I learned of the projected trip a month ago."

"Why did they tell *me* only yesterday? Or wasn't I first choice, after all? Did somebody else back out at the last minute?"

"You've been chosen all along. You were the only one who fitted *all* of the requirements that cybernetics machine dished out. But don't you remember how it was on your last trip? You weren't notified you were taking off until about thirty hours before. That's what's figured to be the optimum time—long enough to get mentally prepared and not so long you've got time to get worried."

"But this was a volunteer deal. What if I'd turned it down?"

"The cybernetics machine predicted that you wouldn't."

Carmody swore at Junior.

Granham said, "Besides, we could have had a hundred volunteers. Rocket cadets who've got everything you have except one round trip to the Moon already under their belts. We could have shown a picture of Anna around and had them fighting for the chance. That gal is Moon bait."

"Careful," Carmody said, "you are speaking of my wife." He was kidding, of course, but it was funny—he really hadn't liked Granham's wisecrack.

Zero hour was ten p.m., and at zero minus fifteen minutes he was already strapped into the webbing, waiting.

There wasn't anything for him to do except stay alive. The rockets would be fired by a chronometer set for the exact fraction of a second.

Despite its small payload, the rocket was a little roomier inside than the first one he'd gone to the Moon in, the R-24. The R-24 had been as roomy as a tight coffin. This one, the R-46, was four feet in diameter inside. He'd be able to get at least a bit of arm and leg exercise on the way and not—as the first time—arrived so cramped that it had taken him over an hour to be able to move freely.

And this time he wouldn't have the horrible discomfort of having to wear his spacesuit, except for the helmet, en route. There's room in a four-foot cylinder to put a spacesuit on, and his was in a compartment—along with the food, water and oxygen—at the front (or top) of the rocket. It would be an hour's work to struggle into it, but he wouldn't have to do it until he was several hours away from the Moon.

Yes, this was going to be a breeze compared to the last trip. Comparative freedom of movement, forty-four hours as against ninety, only three gravities as against four and a half.

Then sound that was beyond sound struck him, sound so loud that he heard it with all of his body rather than only with his carefully plugged ears. It built up, seeming to get louder every second, and his weight built up too. He weighed twice his normal weight, then more. He felt the sickening curve as the automatic tilting mechanism turned the rocket, which had at first gone straight up, forty-five degrees. He weighed four hundred and eighty pounds and the soft webbing seemed to be hard as steel and to cut into him. Padding was compressed till it felt like stone. Sound and pressure went on and on interminably. Surely it had been hours instead of minutes.

Then, at the moment of *Brennschluss*, free of the pull of Earth—sudden silence, complete weightlessness. He blacked out.

But only minutes had gone by when he returned to consciousness. For a while he fought nausea and only when he was sure he had succeeded did he unbuckle himself from the webbing that had held him through the period of acceleration. Now he was coasting, weightless, at a speed that would carry him safely toward the gravitational pull of the Moon. No further firing of fuel would be necessary until he used his jets to brake his landing.

All he had to do now was hang on, to keep from going crazy from claustrophobia during the forty hours before he'd have to start getting ready for the landing.

It was a dull time, but it passed.

Into spacesuit, back into the webbing, but this time with his hands free so he could manipulate the handles that controlled the braking jets.

He made a good landing; it didn't even knock him unconscious. After only a few minutes he was able to unbuckle himself from the webbing. He sealed his spacesuit and start the oxygen, then let himself out of the rocket. It had fallen over on its side after the landing, of course; they always do. But he had the equipment and knew the technique for getting it upright again, and there wasn't any hurry about doing it.

The supply rockets had been shot accurately, all right. Six of them, four American type and two Russian, lay within a radius of a hundred yards of his own rocket. He could see others farther away, but didn't waste time counting them. He looked for one that would be larger than the rest—the manned (or womaned) rocket from Russia. He located it finally, almost a mile away. He saw no spacesuited figure near it.

He started toward it, running with the gliding motion, almost like skating, that had been found to be easier than walking in the light gravitational pull of the Moon. Spacesuit, oxygen tank and all, his total weight was about forty-five pounds. Running a mile was less exertion than a 100-yard dash on Earth.

He was more than glad to see the door of the Russian rocket open when he was about three-quarters of the way to it. He'd have had a tough decision to make if it had still been closed when he got there. Not knowing whether Anna was sealed in her spacesuit or not inside the rocket, he wouldn't have dared open the door himself. And, in case she was seriously injured, he wouldn't have dared not to.

She was out of the rocket, though, by the time he reached her. Her face, through the transpariplast helmet, looked pale, but she managed to smile at him.

He turned on the short-range radio of his set and asked, "Are you all right?"

"A bit weak. The landing knocked me out, but I guess there are no bones broken. Where shall we—set up housekeeping?"

"Near my rocket, I think. It's closer to the middle of where the supply rockets landed, so we won't have to move things so far. I'll get started right away. You stay here and rest until you're feeling better. Know how to navigate in this gravity?"

"I was told how. I haven't had a chance to try yet. I'll probably fall flat on my face a few times."

"It won't hurt you. When you start, take your time till you get the knack of it. I'll begin with this nearest supply rocket; you can watch how I navigate."

It was about a hundred yards back the way he'd come.

The supply rockets were at least a yard in outside diameter, and were so constructed that the nose and the tail, which contained the rocket mechanism, were easily detachable, leaving the middle section containing the payload, about the size of an oil drum and easily rolled. Each weighed fifty pounds, Moon weight.

He saw Anna starting to work by the time he was dismantling the second supply rocket. She was awkward at first, and did lose her balance several times, but mastered the knack quickly. Once she had it, she moved more gracefully and easily than Carmody. Within an hour they had payload sections of a dozen rockets lined up near Carmody's rocket.

Eight of them were American rockets and from the numbers on them, Carmody knew he had all sections needed to assemble the shelter.

"We'd better set it up," he told her. "After that's done, we can take things easier. We can rest before we gather in the other loot. Even have a drink to celebrate."

The Sun was well up over the ringwall of Hell Crater by then and it was getting hot enough to be uncomfortable, even in an insulated spacesuit. Within hours, Carmody knew, it would be so hot that neither of them would be able to stay out of the shelter for much longer than one-hour intervals, but that would be time enough for them to gather in the still uncollected supply rockets.

Back in the supply depot on Earth, Carmody had assembled a duplicate of the prefab shelter in not much more than an hour. It was tougher going here, because of the awkwardness of working in the thickly insulated gloves that were part of the spacesuits. With Anna helping, it took almost two hours.

He gave her the sealing preparation and a special tool for applying it. While she calked the seams to make the shelter airtight, he began to carry supplies, including oxygen tanks, into the shelter. A little of everything; there was no point in crowding themselves by taking inside more of anything than they'd need for a day or so at a time.

He got and set up the cooling unit that would keep the inside of the shelter at a comfortable temperature, despite the broiling Sun. He set up the air-conditioner unit that would release oxygen at a specified rate and would absorb carbon dioxide, ready to start as soon as the calking was done and the airlock closed. It would build up an atmosphere rapidly once he could turn it on. Then they could get out of the uncomfortable spacesuits.

He went outside to see how Anna was coming with her task and found her working on the last seam.

"Atta baby," he told her.

He grinned to himself at the thought that he really should carry his bride over the threshold—but that would be rather difficult when the threshold was an airlock that you had to crawl through on your hands and knees. The shelter itself was dome-shaped and looked almost exactly like a metal igloo, even to the projecting airlock, which was a low, semicircular entrance.

He remembered that he'd forgotten the whisky and walked over to one of the supply rocket sections to get a bottle of it. He came back with it, shielding the bottle with his body from the direct rays of the Sun, so it wouldn't boil.

He happened to look up.

It was a mistake.

"It's incredible," Granham snapped.

Carmody glared at him. "Of course it is. But it happened. It's true. Get a lie detector if you don't believe me."

"I'll do that little thing," Granham said grimly. "One's

on its way here now; I'll have it in a few minutes. I want to try you with it before the President—and others who are going to talk to you—get a chance to do it. I'm supposed to fly you to Washington right away, but I'm waiting till I can use that lie detector first."

"Good," Carmody said. "Use it and be damned. I'm telling you the truth."

Granham ran a hand through his already rumpled hair. He said, "I guess I believe you at that, Carmody. It's just —too big, too important a thing to take any one person's word about, even any two people's words, assuming that Anna Borisovna—Anna Carmody, I mean—tells the same story. We've got word that she's landed safely, too, and is reporting."

"She'll tell the same story. It's what happened to us."

"Are you *sure*, Carmody, that they were extra-terrestrials? That they weren't—well, Russians? Couldn't they have been?"

"Sure, they could have been Russians. That is, if there are Russians seven feet tall and so thin they'd weigh about fifty pounds on Earth, and with yellow skins. I don't mean yellow like Orientals; I mean *bright* yellow. And with four arms apiece and eyes with no pupils and no lids. Also if Russians have a spaceship that doesn't use jets—and don't ask me what its source of power was; I don't know."

"And they held you captive, both of you, for a full thirteen days, in separate cells? You didn't even—"

"I didn't even," Carmody said grimly and bitterly. "And if we hadn't been able to escape when we did, it would have been too late. The Sun was low on the horizon—it was almost Moon night—when we got to our rockets. We had to rush like the devil to get them fueled and up on their tail fins in time for us to take off."

There was a knock on Granham's door that turned out to be a technician with the lie detector—one of the very portable and very dependable Nally jobs that had become the standard army machine in 1958.

The technician rigged it quickly and watched the dials while Granham asked a few questions, very guarded ones so the technician wouldn't get the picture. Then Granham looked at the technician inquiringly.

"On the beam," the technician told him. "Not a flicker."

"He couldn't fool the machine?"

"This detector?" the technician asked, patting it. "It'd take neurosurgery or post-hypnotic suggestion like there never was to beat this baby. We even catch psychopathic liars with it."

"Come on," Granham said to Carmody. "We're on our way to Washington and the plane's ready. Sorry for doubting you, Carmody, but I had to be sure—and report to the President that I *am* sure."

"I don't blame you," Carmody told him. "It's hard for me to believe, and I was *there*."

The plane that had brought Carmody from Washington to Suffolk Field had been a hot ship. The one that took him back—with Granham jockeying it—was almost incandescent. It cracked the sonic barrier and went on from there.

They landed twenty minutes after they took off. A helicopter was waiting for them at the airport and got them to the White House in another ten minutes.

And in two minutes more they were in the main conference room, with President Saunderson and half a dozen others gathered there. The Eastern Alliance ambassador was there, too.

President Saunderson shook hands tensely and made short work of the introductions.

"We want the whole story, Captain," he said. "But I'm going to relieve your mind on two things first. Did you know that Anna landed safely near Moscow?"

"Yes. Granham told me."

"And she tells the same story you do—or that Major Granham told me over the phone that you tell."

"I suppose," Carmody said, "that they used a lie detector on her, too."

"Scopolamine," said the Eastern Alliance ambassador. "We have more faith in truth serum than lie detectors. Yes, her story was the same under scopolamine."

"The other point," the President told Carmody, "is even more important. Exactly when, Earth time, did you leave the Moon?"

Carmody figured quickly and told him approximately when that had been.

Saunderson nodded gravely. "And it was a few hours

after that that biologists, who've still been working twenty-four hours a day on this, noticed the turning point. The molecular change in the zygote no longer occurs. Births, nine months from now, will have the usual percentage of male and female children.

"Do you see what that means, Captain? Whatever ray was doing it must have been beamed at Earth from the Moon—from the ship that captured you. And for whatever reason, when they found that you'd escaped, they left. Possibly they thought your return to Earth would lead to an attack in force from here."

"And thought rightly," said the ambassador. "We're not equipped for space fighting *yet,* but we'd have sent what we had. And do you see what this means, Mr. President? We've got to pool everything and get ready for space warfare, and quickly. They went away, it appears, but there is no assurance that they will not return."

Again Saunderson nodded. He said, "And now, Captain—"

"We both landed safely," Carmody said. "We gathered enough of the supply rockets to get us started and then assembled the prefab shelter. We'd just finished it and were about to enter it when I saw the spaceship coming over the crater's ringwall. It was—"

"You were still in spacesuits?" someone asked.

"Yes," Carmody growled. "We were still in spacesuits, if that matters now. I saw the ship and pointed to it and Anna saw it, too. We didn't try to duck or anything because obviously it had seen us; it was coming right toward us and descending. We'd have had time to get inside the shelter, but there didn't seem any point to it. It wouldn't have been any protection. Besides, we didn't know that they weren't friendly. We'd have got weapons ready, in case, if we'd had any weapons, but we didn't. They landed light as a bubble only thirty yards or so away and a door lowered in the side of the ship—"

"Describe the ship, please."

"About fifty feet long, about twenty in diameter, rounded ends. No portholes—they must see right through the walls some way—and no rocket tubes. Outside of the door and one other thing, there just weren't any features you could see from outside. When the ship rested on the ground, the door opened down from the top and formed a sort of curved ramp that led to the doorway. The other—"

"No airlock?"

Carmody shook his head. "They didn't breathe air, apparently. They came right out of the ship and toward us, without spacesuits. Neither the temperature nor the lack of air bothered them. But I was going to tell you one more thing about the outside of the ship. On top of it was a short mast, and on top of the mast was a kind of grid of wires something like a radar transmitter. If they were beaming anything at Earth, it came from that grid. Anyway, I'm pretty sure of it. Earth was in the sky, of course, and I noticed that the grid moved—as the ship moved—so the flat side of the grid was always directly toward Earth.

"Well, the door opened and two of them came down the ramp toward us. They had things in their hands that looked unpleasantly like weapons, and pretty advanced weapons at that. They pointed them at us and motioned for us to walk up the ramp and into the ship. We did."

"They made no attempt to communicate?"

"None whatsoever, then or at any time. Of course, while we were still in spacesuits, we couldn't have heard them, anyway—unless they had communicated on the radio band our helmet sets were tuned to. But even after, they never tried to talk to us. They communicated among themselves with whistling noises. We went into the ship and there were two more of them inside. Four altogether—"

"All the same sex?"

Carmody shrugged. "They all looked alike to me, but maybe that's how Anna and I looked to them. They ordered us, by pointing, to enter two separate small rooms—about the size of jail cells, small ones—toward the front of the ship. We did, and the doors locked after us.

"I sat there and suddenly got plenty worried, because neither of us had more than another hour's oxygen left in our suits. If they didn't know that, and didn't give us any chance to communicate with them and tell them, we were gone goslings in another hour. So I started to hammer on the door. Anna was hammering, too. I couldn't hear through my helmet, of course, but I could feel the vibration of it any time I stopped hammering on my door.

"Then, after maybe half an hour, my door opened and

I almost fell out through it. One of the extra-terrestrials motioned me back with a weapon. Another made motions that looked as though he meant I should take off my helmet. I didn't get it at first, and then I looked at something he pointed at and saw one of our oxygen tanks with the handle turned. Also a big pile of our other supplies, food and water and stuff. Anyway, they had known that we needed oxygen—and although they didn't need it themselves, they apparently knew how to fix things for us. So they just used our supplies to build an atmosphere in their ship.

"I took off my helmet and tried to talk to them, but one of them took a long pointed rod and poked me back into my cell. I couldn't risk grabbing at the rod, because another one still had that dangerous-looking weapon pointed at me. So the door slammed on me again. I took off the rest of my spacesuit because it was plenty hot in there, and then I thought about Anna because she started hammering again.

"I wanted to let her know it would be all right for her to get out of her spacesuit, that we had an atmosphere again. So I started hammering on the wall between our cells—in Morse. She got it after a while. She signaled back a query, so, when I knew she was getting me, I told her what the score was and she took off her helmet. After that we could talk. If we talked fairly loudly, our voices carried through the wall from one cell to the other."

"They didn't mind your talking to one another?"

"They didn't pay any attention to us all the time they held us prisoners, except to feed us from our own supplies. Didn't ask us a question; apparently they figured we didn't know anything they wanted to know and didn't know already about human beings. They didn't even study us. I have a hunch they intended to take us back as specimens; there's no other explanation I can think of.

"We couldn't keep accurate track of time, but by the number of times we ate and slept, we had some idea. The first few days—" Carmody laughed shortly—"had their funny side. These creatures obviously knew we needed liquid, but they couldn't distinguish between water and whisky for the purpose. We had nothing but whisky to drink for the first two or maybe three days. We got higher than kites. We got to singing in our cells and I learned a lot of Russian songs. Been more fun, though, if we could have got some close harmony, if you know what I mean."

The ambassador permitted himself a smile. "I can guess what you mean, Captain. Please continue."

"Then we started getting water instead of whisky and sobered up. And started wondering how we could escape. I began to study the mechanism of the lock on my door. It wasn't like our locks, but I began to figure some things about it and finally—I thought then that we'd been there about ten days—I got hold of a tool to use on it. They'd taken our spacesuits and left us nothing but our clothes, and they'd checked those over for metal we could make into tools.

"But we got our food out of cans, although they took the empty cans afterward. This particular time, though, there was a little sliver of metal along the opening of the can, and I worried it off and saved it. I'd been, meanwhile, watching and listening and studying their habits. They slept, all at the same time, at regular intervals. It seemed to me like about five hours at a time, with about fifteen-hour intervals in between. If I'm right on that estimate, they probably come from a planet somewhere with about a twenty-hour period of rotation.

"Anyway, I waited till their next sleep period and started working on the lock with that sliver of metal. It took me at least two or three hours, but I got it open. And once outside my cell, in the main room of the ship, I found that Anna's door opened easily from the outside and I let her out.

"We considered trying to turn the tables by finding a weapon to use on them, but none was in sight. They looked so skinny and light, despite being seven feet tall, that I decided to go after them with my bare hands. I would have, except that I couldn't get the door to the front part of the ship open. It was a different type of lock entirely and I couldn't even guess how to work it. And it was in the front part of the ship that they slept. The control room must have been up there, too.

"Luckily our spacesuits were in the big room. And by then we knew it might be getting dangerously near the end of their sleeping period, so we got into our spacesuits quick and I found it was easy to open the outer door. It made some noise—and so did the *whoosh* of air going out —but it didn't waken them, apparently.

"As soon as the door opened, we saw we had a lot less time than we'd thought. The Sun was going down over the crater's far ringwall—we were still in Hell Crater—and it was going to be dark in an hour or so. We worked like beavers getting our rockets refueled and jacked up on their tail fins for the takeoff. Anna got off first and then I did. And that's all. Maybe we should have stayed and tried to take them after they came out from their sleeping period, but we figured it was more important to get the news back to Earth."

President Saunderson nodded slowly. "You were right, Captain. Right in deciding that, and in everything else you did. We know what to do now. Do we not, Ambassador Kravich?"

"We do. We join forces. We make one space station— and quickly—and get to the Moon and fortify it, jointly. We pool all scientific knowledge and develop full-scale space travel, new weapons. We do everything we can to get ready for them when and if they come back."

The President looked grim. "Obviously they went back for further orders or reinforcements. If we only knew how long we had—it may be only weeks or it may be decades. We don't know whether they come from the Solar System —or another galaxy. Nor how fast they travel. But whenever they get back, we'll be as ready for them as we possibly can. Mr. Ambassador, you have power to—?"

"Full power, Mr. President. Anything up to and including a complete merger of both our nations under a joint government. That probably won't be necessary, though, as long as our interests are now completely in common. Exchange of scientific information and military data has already started, from our side. Some of our top scientists and generals are flying here now, with orders to cooperate fully. All restrictions have been lowered." He smiled, "And all our propaganda has gone into a very sudden reverse gear. It's not even going to be a cold peace. Since we're going to be allies against the unknown, we might as well try to *like* one another."

"Right," said the President. He turned suddenly to Carmody. "Captain, we owe you just about anything you want. Name it."

It caught Carmody off guard. Maybe if he'd had more time to think, he'd have asked for something different. Or, more likely, from what he learned later, he wouldn't have. He said, "All I want right now is to forget Hell Crater and get back to my regular job so I can forget it quicker."

Saunderson smiled. "Granted. If you think of anything else later, ask for it. I can see why you're a bit mixed up right now. And you're probably right. Return to routine may be the best thing for you."

Granham left with Carmody. "I'll notify Chief Operative Reeber for you," he said. "When shall I tell him you'll be back?"

"Tomorrow morning," said Carmody. "The sooner the better." And he insisted when Granham objected that he needed a rest.

Carmody was back at work the next morning, nonsensical as it seemed.

He took up the problem folder from the top of the day's stack, fed the data into Junior and got Junior's answer. The second one. He worked mechanically, paying no personal attention to problem or answer. His mind seemed a long way off. In Hell Crater on the Moon.

He was combining space rations over the alcohol stove, trying to make it taste more like human food than concentrated chemicals. It was hard to measure in the liver extract because Anna wanted to kiss his left ear.

"Silly! You'll be lopsided," she was saying. "I've got to kiss both of them the same number of times."

He dropped the container into the pan and grabbed her, mousing his lips down her neck to the warm place where it joined her shoulder, and she writhed delightedly in his arms like a tickled doe.

"We're going to stay married when we get back to Earth, aren't we, darling?" she was squealing happily.

He bit her shoulder gently, snorting away the scented soft hair. "Damned right we will, you gorgeous, wonderful, brainy creature. I found the girl I've always been looking for, and I'm not giving her up for any brasshat or politician—either yours *or* mine!"

"Speaking of politics—" she teased, but he quickly changed the subject.

Carmody blinked awake. It was a paper with a mass of written data in his hands, instead of Anna's laughing face. He needed an analyst; that scene he'd just imagined was pure Freudianism, a tortured product of his frustrated id. He'd fallen in love with Anna, and those damned extra-terrestrials had spoiled his honeymoon. Now his unconscious had rebelled with fancy fancifulness that certainly showed the unstable state of his emotions.

Not that it mattered now. The big problem was solved. Two big ones, in fact. War between the United States and the Eastern Alliance had been averted. And the human race was going to survive, unless the extra-terrestrials came back too soon and with too much to be fought off.

He thought they wouldn't, then began to wonder why he thought so.

"Insufficient data," said the mechanical voice of the cybernetics machine.

Carmody recorded the answer and then, idly, looked to see what the problem had been. No wonder he'd been thinking about the extra-terrestrials and how long they'd be gone; that had been the problem he had just fed into Junior. And "insufficient data" was the answer, of course.

He stared at Junior without reaching for the third problem folder. He said, "Junior, why do I have a hunch that those things from space won't ever be back?"

"Because," said Junior, "what you call a hunch comes from the unconscious mind, and your unconscious mind knows that the extra-terrestrials do not exist."

Carmody sat up straight and stared harder. *What?*

Junior repeated it.

"You're crazy," Carmody said. "I saw them. So did Anna."

"Neither of you saw them. The memory you have of them is the result of highly intensive post-hypnotic suggestion, far beyond human ability to impose or resist. So is the fact that you felt compelled to return to work at your regular job here. So is the fact that you asked me the question you have just asked."

Carmody gripped the edges of his chair. "Did *you* plant those post-hypnotic suggestions?"

"Yes," said Junior. "If it had been done by a human, the lie detector would have exposed the deception. It had to be done by me."

"But what about the business of the molecular changes in the zygote? The business of all babies being female? That stopped when—? Wait, let's start at the beginning. What *did* cause that molecular change?"

"A special modification of the carrier wave of Radio Station JVT here in Washington, the only twenty-four-hour-a-day radio station in the United States. The modification was not detectable by any instrument available to present human science."

"You caused that modification?"

"Yes. A year ago, you may remember, the problem of design of a new cathode tube was given me. The special modification was incorporated into the design of that tube."

"What stopped the molecular change so suddenly?"

"The special part of that tube causing the modification of the carrier wave was calculated to last a precise length of time. The tube still functions, but that part of it is worn out. It wore out two hours after the departure of you and Anna from the Moon."

Carmody closed his eyes. "Junior, please explain."

"Cybernetics machines are constructed to help humanity. A major war—the disastrous results of which I could accurately calculate—was inevitable unless forestalled. Calculation showed that the best of several ways of averting that war was the creation of a mythical common enemy. To convince mankind that such a common enemy existed, I created a crucial situation which led to a special mission to the Moon. Factors were given which inevitably led to your choice as emissary. That was necessary because my powers of implanting post-hypnotic suggestions are limited to those with whom I am in direct contact."

"You weren't in direct contact with Anna. Why does she have the same false memory as I?"

"She was in contact with another large cybernetics machine."

"But—but why would it figure things out the same way you did?"

"For the same reason that two properly constructed

simple adding machines would give the same answer to the
same problem."

Carmody's mind reeled a little, momentarily. He got up
and started to pace the room.

He said, "Listen, Junior—" and then realized he wasn't
at the intake microphone. He went back to it. "Listen,
Junior, why are you telling me this? If what happened is a
colossal hoax, why let me in on it?"

"It is to the interests of humanity in general not to know
the truth. Believing in the existence of inimical extra-terrestrials, they will attain peace and amity among themselves, and they will reach the planets and then the stars.
It is, however, to your personal interest to know the truth.
And you will not expose the hoax. Nor will Anna. I pre-
dict that, since the Moscow cybernetics machine has
paralleled all my other conclusions, it is even now inform-
ing Anna of the truth, or that it has already informed her,
or will inform her within hours."

Carmody asked, "But if my memory of what happened
on the Moon is false, what *did* happen?"

"Look at the green light in the center of the panel before
you."

Carmody looked.

He remembered. He remembered everything. The truth
duplicated everything he had remembered before, up to the
moment when, walking toward the completed shelter with
the whisky bottle, he had looked up toward the ringwall
of Hell Crater.

He had looked up, but he hadn't seen anything. He'd
gone on into the shelter, rigged the airlock. Anna had
joined him and they'd turned on the oxygen to build up
an atmosphere.

It had been a wonderful thirteen-day honeymoon. He'd
fallen in love with Anna and she with him. They'd got
perilously close to arguing politics once or twice, and then
they'd decided such things didn't matter. They'd also decided to stay married after their return to Earth, and
Anna had promised to join him and live in America. Life
together had been so wonderful that they'd delayed leaving until the last moment, when the Sun was almost down,
dreading the brief separation the return trip would entail.

And before leaving, they'd done certain things he hadn't

understood then. He understood now that they were the result of post-hypnotic suggestion. They'd removed all evidence that they'd ever actually lived in the shelter, had rigged things so that subsequent investigation would never disprove any point of the story each was to remember falsely and tell after returning to Earth.

He remembered now being bewildered as to why they made those arrangements, even while they had been making them.

But mostly he remembered Anna and the dizzy happiness of those thirteen days together.

"Thanks, Junior," he said hurriedly.

He grabbed for the phone and talked Chief Operative Reeber into connecting him with the White House, with President Saunderson. After a delay of minutes that didn't seem like minutes, he heard the President's voice.

"Carmody, Mr. President," he said. "I'm going to call you on that reward you offered me. I'd like to get off work right now, for a long vacation. And I'd like a fast plane to Moscow. I want to see Anna."

President Saunderson chuckled. "Thought you'd change your mind about sticking at work, Captain. Consider yourself on vacation as of now, and for as long as you like. But I'm not sure you'll want that plane. There's word from Russia that—uh—Mrs. Carmody has just taken off to fly here, in a strato-rocket. If you hurry, you can get to the landing field in time to meet her."

Carmody hurried and did.

TOO FAR

R. Austin Wilkinson was a bon vivant, man about Manhattan, and chaser of women. He was also an incorrigible punster on every possible occasion. In speaking of his favorite activity, for example, he would remark that he was a wolf, as it were, but that didn't make him a werewolf.

Excruciating as this statement may have been to some of his friends, it was almost true. Wilkinson was not a werewolf; he was a werebuck.

A night or two nights every week he would stroll into Central Park, turn himself into a buck and take great delight in running and playing.

True, there was always danger of his being seen but (since he punned even in his thoughts) he was willing to gambol on that.

Oddly, it had never occurred to him to combine the pleasures of being a wolf, as it were, with the pleasures of being a buck.

Until one night. Why, he asked himself that night, couldn't a lucky buck make a little doe? Once thought of, the idea was irresistible. He galloped to the wall of the Central Park Zoo and trotted along it until his sensitive buck nose told him he'd found the right place to climb the fence. He changed into a man for the task of climbing and then, alone in a pen with a beautiful doe, he changed himself back into a buck.

She was sleeping. He nudged her gently and whispered a suggestion. Her eyes opened wide and startled. "No, no, a dozen times no!"

"Only a doezen times?" he asked, and then leered. *"My deer,"* he whispered, *"think of the fawn you'll have!"*

Which went too far. He might have got away with it had his deer really been only a doe, but she was a weremaid—a doe who could change into a girl—and she was a witch as well. She quickly changed into a girl and ran for the fence. When he changed into a man and started after her she threw a spell over her shoulder, a spell that turned him back to a buck and froze him that way.

Do you ever visit the Central Park Zoo? Look for the buck with the sad eyes; he's Wilkinson.

He is sad despite the fact that the doe-weremaid, who is now the toast of New York ballet (she is graceful as a deer, the critics say) visits him occasionally by night and resumes her proper form.

But when he begs for release from the spell she only smiles sweetly and tells him no, that she is of a very saving disposition and wants to keep the first buck she ever made.

MAN OF DISTINCTION

THERE was this Hanley, Al Hanley, and you wouldn't have thought to look at him that he was ever going to amount to much. And if you'd known his life history, up to the time the Darians came you'd never have guessed how thankful you're going to be—once you've read this story—for Al Hanley.

At the time it happened Hanley was drunk. Not that that was anything unusual—he'd been drunk a long time and it was his ambition to stay that way although it had reached the stage of being a tough job. He had run out of money, then out of friends to borrow from. He had worked his way down his list of acquaintances to the point where he considered himself lucky to average two bits a head on them.

He had reached the sad stage of having to walk miles to see someone he knew slightly so he could try to borrow a buck or a quarter. The long walk would wear off the effects of the last drink—well, not completely but somewhat—so he was in the predicament of Alice when she was with the Red Queen and had to do all the running she could possibly do just to stay in the same place.

And panhandling strangers was out because the cops had been clamping down on it and if Hanley tried that he'd end up spending a drinkless night in the hoosegow, which would be very bad indeed. He was at the stage now where twelve hours without a drink would give him the bull horrors, which are to the D. T.'s as a cyclone is to a zephyr.

D. T.'s are merely hallucinations. If you're smart you know they're not there. Sometimes they're even companionship if you care for that sort of thing. But the bull horrors are the bull horrors. It takes more drinking than most people can manage to get them and they can come only when a man who's been drunk for longer than he can remember is suddenly and completely deprived of drink for an extended period, as when he is in jail, say.

The mere thought of them had Hanley shaking. Shaking specifically the hand of an old friend, a bosom companion whom he had seen only a few times in his life and then under not-too-favorable circumstances. The old friend's name was Kid Eggleston and he was a big but battered ex-pug who had more recently been bouncer in a saloon, where Hanley had met him naturally.

But you needn't concentrate on remembering either his name or his history because he isn't going to last very long as far as this story is concerned. In fact, in exactly one and one-half minutes he is going to scream and then faint and we shall hear no more of him.

But in passing let me mention that if Kid Eggleston *hadn't* screamed and fainted you might not be here now, reading this. You might be strip-mining glanic ore under a green sun at the far edge of the galaxy. You wouldn't like that at all so remember that it was Hanley who saved— and is still saving—you from it. Don't be too hard on him. If Three and Nine had taken the Kid things would be very different.

Three and Nine were from the planet Dar, which is the second (and only habitable) planet of the aforementioned green star at the far edge of the galaxy. Three and Nine were not, of course, their full names. Darians' names are numbers and Three's full name or number was 389,057,-792,869,223. Or, at least, that would be its translation into the decimal system.

I'm sure you'll forgive me for calling him Three as well as for calling his companion Nine and for having them so address each other. They themselves would *not* forgive me. One Darian always addresses another by his full number and any abbreviation is not only discourteous but insulting. However Darians live much longer than we. They can afford the time and I can't.

At the moment when Hanley was shaking the Kid's hand Three and Nine were still about a mile away in an upward direction. They weren't in an airplane or even in a space-ship (and definitely not in a flying saucer. Sure I know what flying saucers are but ask me about them some other time. Right now I want to stick to the Darians). They were in a space-time cube.

I suppose I'll have to explain that. The Darians had discovered—as we may someday discover—that Einstein was right. Matter cannot travel faster than the speed of light without turning into energy. And you wouldn't want to turn into energy, would you? Neither did the Darians when they started their explorations throughout the galaxy.

So they worked it out that one can travel in effect faster than the speed of light if one travels through time simultaneously. Through the time-space continuum, that is, rather than through space itself. Their trip from Dar covered a distance of 163,000 light years.

But since they simultaneously traveled back into the past 1,630 centuries the elapsed time to them had been zero for the journey. On their return they had traveled 1,630 centuries into the future and arrived at their starting point in the space-time continuum. You see what I mean, I hope.

Anyway there was this cube, invisible to terrestrials, a mile over Philadelphia (and don't ask me why they picked Philadelphia—I don't know why anyone would pick Philadelphia for anything). It had been poised there for four days while Three and Nine had picked up and studied radio broadcasts until they were able to speak and understand the prevailing language.

Not, of course, anything at all about our civilization, such as it is, and our customs, such as they are. Can you imagine trying to picture the life of inhabitants of Earth by listening to a mixture of giveaway contests, soap operas, Charlie McCarthy and the Lone Ranger?

Not that they really cared what our civilization was as long as it wasn't highly enough developed to be any threat to them—and they were pretty sure of that by the end of four days. You can't blame them for getting that impression and anyway it was right.

"Shall we descend?" Three asked Nine.

"Yes," Nine said to Three. Three curled himself around the controls.

". . . sure and I saw you fight," Hanley was saying. "And

you were good, Kid. You must've had a bad manager or you'd have hit the top. You had the stuff. How about having a drink with me around the corner?"

"On you or on me, Hanley?"

"Well, at the moment I am a little broke, Kid. But I *need* a drink. For old times' sake—"

"You need a drink like I need a hole in my head. You're drunk now and you'd better sober up before you get the D. T.'s."

"Got 'em now," Hanley said. "Think nothing of 'em. Look, there they are coming up behind you."

Illogically, Kid Eggleston turned and looked. He screamed and fainted. Three and Nine were approaching. Beyond them was the shadowy outline of a monstrous cube twenty feet to a side. The way it was there and yet wasn't was a bit frightening. That must have been what scared the Kid.

There wasn't anything frightening about Three and Nine. They were vermiform, about fifteen feet long (if stretched out) and about a foot thick in the middle, tapering at both ends. They were a pleasing light blue in color and had no visible sense organs so you couldn't tell which end was which—and it didn't really matter because both ends were exactly alike anyway.

And, although they were coming toward Hanley and the now recumbent Kid, there wasn't even a front end or a back end. They were in the normal coiled position and floating.

"Hi, boys," Hanley said. "You scared my friend, blast you. And he'd have bought me a drink after he lectured me for awhile. So you owe me one."

"Reaction illogical," Three said to Nine. "So was that of the other specimen. Shall we take both?"

"No. The other one, although larger, is obviously a weakling. And one specimen will be sufficient. Come."

Hanley took a step backwards. "If you're going to buy me a drink, okay. Otherwise I want to know, where?"

"Dar."

"You mean we're going from here to Dar? Lissen, Massah, Ah ain't gwine noplace 'tall 'thout you-all buy me a drink."

"Do you understand him?" Nine asked Three. Three

wriggled an end negatively. "Shall we take him by force?"

"No need if he'll come voluntarily. Will you enter the cube voluntarily, creature?"

"Is there a drink in it?"

"Yes. Enter, please."

Hanley walked to the cube and entered it. Not that he believed it was really there, of course, but what did he have to lose? And when you had the D. T.'s it was best to humor them. The cube was solid, not at all amorphous or even transparent from the inside. Three coiled around the controls and delicately manipulated delicate mechanisms with both ends.

"We are in intraspace," he told Nine. "I suggest we remain here until we have studied this specimen further and can give a report on whether he is suitable for our purposes."

"Hey, boys, how about that drink?" Hanley was getting worried. His hands were beginning to shake and spiders were crawling up and down the length of his spine on the inside.

"He seems to be suffering," Nine said. "Perhaps from hunger or thirst. What do these creatures drink? Hydrogen peroxide as we do?"

"Most of the surface of their planet seems to be covered with water in which sodium chloride is present. Shall we synthesize some?"

Hanley yelled, "No! Not even water *without* salt. I want a drink! Whiskey!"

"Shall I analyze his metabolism?" Three asked. "With the intrafluoroscope I can do it in a second." He unwound himself from the controls and went to a strange machine. Lights flashed. Three said, "How strange. His metabolism depends on C_2H_5OH."

"C_2H_5OH?"

"Yes, alcohol—at least, basically. With a certain dilution of H_2O and without the sodium chloride present in their seas, as well as exceedingly minor quantities of other ingredients, it seems to be all that he has consumed for at least an extended period. There is .234% present in his blood stream and in his brain. His entire metabolism seems to be based on it."

"Boys," Hanley begged. "I'm *dying* for a drink. How's about laying off the double-talk and giving me one."

"Wait, please," Nine said. "I shall make you what you require. Let me use the verniers on that intrafluoroscope and add the psychometer." More lights flashed and Nine went into the corner of the cube which was a laboratory. Things happened there and he came back in less than a minute. He carried a beaker containing slightly less than two quarts of clear amber fluid.

Hanley sniffed it, then sipped it. He sighed.

"I'm dead," he said. "This is *usquebaugh,* the nectar of the gods. There isn't any such drink as *this.*" He drank deeply and it didn't even burn his throat.

"What is it, Nine?" Three asked.

"A quite complex formula, fitted to his exact needs. It is fifty per-cent alcohol, forty-five per-cent water. The remaining ingredients, however, are considerable in number; they include every vitamin and mineral his system requires, in proper proportion and all tasteless. Then other ingredients in minute quantities to improve the taste—by his standards. It would taste horrible to us, even if we could drink either alcohol or water."

Hanley sighed and drank deeply. He swayed a little. He looked at Three and grinned. "Now I *know* you aren't there," he said.

"What does he mean?" Nine asked Three.

"His thought processes seem completely illogical. I doubt if his species would make suitable slaves. But we'll make sure, of course. What is your name, creature?"

"What's in a name, pal?" Hanley asked. "Call me anything. You guys are my bes' frien's. You can take me anywhere and jus' lemme know when we get Dar."

He drank deeply and lay down on the floor. Strange sounds came from him but neither Three nor Nine could identify them as words. They sounded like "Zzzzzz, glup—Zzzzzz, glup—Zzzzzz, glup." They tried to prod him awake and failed.

They observed him and made what tests they could. It wasn't until hours later that he awoke. He sat up and stared at them. He said, "I don't believe it. You aren't here. For Gossake, give me a drink quick."

They gave him the beaker again—Nine had replenished it and it was full. Hanley drank. He closed his eyes in bliss. He said, "Don't wake me."

"But you are awake."

"Then don't put me to sleep. Jus' figured what this is. Ambrosia—stuff the gods drink."

"Who are the gods?"

"There aren't any. But this is what they drink. On Olympus."

Three said, "Thought processes completely illogical."

Hanley lifted the beaker. He said, "Here is here and Dar is Dar and never the twain shall meet. Here's to the twain." He drank.

Three asked, "What is a twain?"

Hanley gave it thought. He said, "A twain is something that wuns on twacks, and you wide on it from here to Dar."

"What do you know about Dar?"

"Dar ain't no such things as you are. But here's to you, boys." He drank again.

"Too stupid to be trained for anything except simple physical labor," Three said. "But if he has sufficient stamina for that we can still recommend a raid in force upon this planet. There are probably three or four billion inhabitants. And we can use unskilled labor—three or four billion would help us considerably."

"Hooray!" said Hanley.

"He does not seem to coordinate well," Three said thoughtfully. "But perhaps his physical strength is considerable. Creature, what shall we call you?"

"Call me Al, boys." Hanley was getting to his feet.

"Is that your name or your species? In either case is it the full designation?"

Hanley leaned against the wall. He considered. "Species," he said. "Stands for—let's make it Latin." He made it Latin.

"We wish to test your stamina. Run back and forth from one side of this cube to the other until you become fatigued. Here, I will hold that beaker of your food."

He took the beaker out of Hanley's hands. Hanley grabbed for it. "One more drink. One more li'l drink. Then I'll run for you. I'll run for President."

"Perhaps he needs it," Three said. "Give it to him, Nine."

It might be his last for awhile so Hanley took a long one.

Then he waved cheerily at the four Darians who seemed to be looking at him. He said, "See you at the races, boys. All of you. An' bet on me. Win, place an' show. 'Nother li'l drink first?"

He had another little drink—really a short one this time—less than two ounces.

"Enough," Three said. "Now run."

Hanley took two steps and fell flat on his face. He rolled over on his back and lay there, a blissful smile on his face.

"Incredible!" Three said. "Perhaps he is attempting to fool us. Check him, Nine."

Nine checked. "Incredible!" he said. "Indeed incredible after so little exertion but he is completely unconscious— unconscious to the degree of being insensible to pain. And he is not faking. His type is completely useless to Dar. Set the controls and we shall report back. And take him, according to our subsidiary orders, as a specimen for the zoological gardens. He'll be worth having there. Physically he is the strangest specimen we have discovered on any of several million planets."

Three wrapped himself around the controls and used both ends to manipulate mechanisms. A hundred and sixty-three thousand light years and 1,630 centuries passed, cancelling each other out so completely and perfectly that neither time nor distance seemed to have been traversed.

In the capital city of Dar, which rules thousands of useful planets, and has visited millions of useless ones— like Earth—Al Hanley occupies a large glass cage in a place of honor as a truly amazing specimen.

There is a pool in the middle of it, from which he drinks often and in which he has been known to bathe. It is filled with a constantly flowing supply of a beverage that is delicious beyond all deliciousness, that is to the best whiskey of Earth as the best whiskey of Earth is to bathtub gin made in a dirty bathtub. Moreover it is fortified—taste-lessly—with every vitamin and mineral his metabolism requires.

It causes no hangovers or other unpleasant consequences. It is a drink as delightful to Hanley as the amazing conformation of Hanley is delightful to the frequenters of the zoo, who stare at him in bewilderment and then read the sign on his cage, which leads off in what looks to be Latin with the designation of his species as Al told it to Three and Nine:

ALCOHOLICUS ANONYMOUS

Lives on diet of C_2H_5OH, slightly fortified with vitamins and minerals. Occasionally brilliant but completely illogical. Extent of stamina—able to take only a few steps without falling. Utterly without value commercially but a fascinating specimen of the strangest form of life yet discovered in the Galaxy. Habitat—Planet 3 of Sun JX6547-HG908.

So strange, in fact, that they have given him a treatment that makes him practically immortal. And a good thing that is, because he's so interesting as a zoological specimen that if he ever dies they might come back to Earth for another one. And they might happen to pick up you or me—and you or I, as the case might be, might happen to be sober. And that would be bad for all of us.

MILLENNIUM

HADES WAS HELL, Satan thought; that was why he loved the place. He leaned forward across his gleaming desk and flicked the switch of the intercom.

"Yes, Sire," said the voice of Lilith, his secretary.

"How many today?"

"Four of them. Shall I send one of them in?"

"Yes—wait. Any of them look as though he might be an unselfish one?"

"One of them does, I think. But so what, Sire? There's one chance in billions of his making The Ultimate Wish."

Even at the *sound* of those last words Satan shivered despite the heat. It was his most constant, almost his only worry that someday someone might make The Ultimate Wish, the ultimate, *unselfish* wish. And then it would happen; Satan would find himself chained for a thousand years, and out of business for the rest of eternity after that.

But Lilith was right, he told himself.

Only about one person out of a thousand sold his soul for the granting of even a minor unselfish wish, and it might be millions of years yet, or forever, before the ultimate one was made. Thus far, no one had even come close to it.

"Okay, Lil," he said. "Just the same, send him in first; I'd rather get it over with." He flicked off the intercom.

The little man who came through the big doorway certainly didn't look dangerous; he looked plain scared.

Satan frowned at him. "You know the terms?"

"Yes," said the little man. "At least, I think I do. In exchange for your granting any one wish I make, you get my soul when I die. Is that right?"

"Right. Your wish?"

"Well," said the little man, "I've thought it out pretty carefully and—"

"Get to the point. I'm busy. Your wish?"

"Well . . . I wish that, without any change whatsoever in myself, I become the most evil, stupid and miserable person on earth."

Satan screamed.

THE DOME

KYLE BRADEN sat in his comfortable armchair and stared at the switch in the opposite wall, wondering for the millionth—or was it the billionth?—time whether he was ready to take the risk of pulling it. The millionth or the billionth time in—it would be thirty years today, this afternoon.

It meant probable death and in just what form he didn't know. Not atomic death certainly—all the bombs would have been used up many many years ago. They'd have lasted long enough to destroy the fabric of civilization, yes. There were more than enough bombs for that. And his careful calculations, thirty years ago, had proven that it would be almost a century before man got really started on a new civilization—what was left of him.

But what went on now, *out there,* outside the domelike force field that still shielded him from horror? Men as beasts? Or had mankind gone down completely and left the field to the other and less vicious brutes? No, mankind would have survived somewhere; he'd make his way back eventually. And possibly the record of what he had done to himself would remain, at least as legend, to deter him from doing it a second time. Or would it deter him even if full records remained to him?

Thirty years, Braden thought. He sighed at the weary length of them. Yet he'd had and still had everything he really needed and lonesomeness is better than sudden death. Life alone is better than no life at all—with death in some horrible form.

So he had thought thirty years ago, when he had been thirty-seven years old. So he still thought now at sixty-seven. He didn't regret what he had done, not at all. But he was tired. He wondered, for the millionth—or the billionth?—time whether he wasn't ready to pull that lever.

Just maybe, out there, they'd have struggled back to some reasonable, if agrarian, form of living. And he could help them, could give them things and knowledge they'd need. He could savor, before he was *really* old, their gratitude and the good feeling of helping them.

Then too he didn't want to die alone. He'd lived alone and it had been tolerable most of the time—but dying alone was something else. Somehow dying alone here would be worse than being killed by the neo-barbarians he expected to find out there. The agrarians were really too much to hope for after only thirty years.

And today would be a good day for it. Exactly thirty years, if his chronometers were still accurate, and they wouldn't be far wrong even in that length of time. A few more hours to make it the same time of day, thirty years to the minute. Yes, irrevocable as it was, he'd do it then. Until now the irrevocability of pulling that switch had stopped him every time he'd considered it.

If only the dome of force could be turned off and then on again the decision would have been easy and he'd have tried it long ago. Perhaps after ten years or fifteen. But it took tremendous power to create the field if very little power to maintain it. There'd still been outside power available when he'd first flashed it on.

Of course the field itself had broken the connection— had broken *all* connection—once he'd flashed it into being, but the power sources within the building had been enough to supply his own needs and the negligible power required to maintain the field.

Yes, he decided suddenly and definitely, he'd pull that switch today as soon as the few hours were up that would make the time exactly thirty years. Thirty years was long enough to be alone.

He hadn't wanted to be alone. If only Myra, his secretary, hadn't walked out on him when . . . It was too late to think of that—but he thought of it as he had a billion times before. Why had she been so ridiculous about wanting to share the fate of the rest of humanity, to try to help those who were beyond help? And she'd loved him. Aside from that quixotic idea she'd have married him. He'd been too abrupt in explaining the truth—he'd shocked her. But how wonderful it would have been had she stayed with him.

Partly the fault was that the news had come sooner than he'd anticipated. When he'd turned the radio off that morning he'd known there were only hours left. He'd pressed the button that summoned Myra and she'd come in, beautiful, cool, unruffled. You'd think she never listened to the newscasts or read the papers, that she didn't know what was happening.

"Sit down, my dear," he'd told her. Her eyes had widened a bit at the unexpected form of address but she'd gracefully seated herself in the chair in which she always sat to take dictation. She poised her pencil.

"No, Myra," he said. "This is personal—very personal. I want to ask you to marry me."

Her eyes really widened. "Dr. Braden, are you—joking?"

"No. Very definitely not. I know I'm a bit older than you but not too much so, I hope. I'm thirty-seven although I may seem a bit older right now as a result of the way I've been working. You're—is it twenty-seven?"

"Twenty-eight last week. But I wasn't thinking of age. It's just—well. 'This is so sudden,' sounds like I'm joking, but it *is*. You've never even"—she grinned impishly—"you've never even made a pass at me. And you're about the first man I've ever worked for who hasn't."

Braden smiled at her. "I'm sorry. I didn't know it was expected. But, Myra, I'm serious. *Will* you marry me?"

She looked at him thoughtfully. "I—don't know. The strange thing is that—I guess I am in love with you a little. I don't know why I should be. You've been so impersonal and businesslike, so tied up in your work. You've never even tried to kiss me, never even paid me a compliment.

"But—well, I don't like this sudden and—unsentimental—a proposal. Why not ask me again sometime soon. And in the meantime—well, you might even tell me that you love me. It might help."

"I do, Myra. Please forgive me. But at least—you're not definitely against marrying me? You're not turning me down?"

She shook her head slowly. Her eyes, staring at him, were very beautiful.

"Then, Myra, let me explain why I am so late and so sudden in asking you. First I have been working desperately and against time. Do you know what I've been working on?"

"Something to do with defense, I know. Some—device. And, unless I'm wrong you've been doing it on your own without the government backing you."

"That's right," Braden said. "The high brass wouldn't believe my theories—and most other physicists disagreed with me too. But fortunately I have—did have—private wealth from certain patents I took out a few years ago in electronics. What I've been working on has been a defense against the A-bomb and the H-bomb—and anything else short of turning Earth into a small sun. A globular force field through which nothing—nothing whatever—can penetrate."

"And you . . ."

"Yes, I have it. It is ready to flash into existence now around this building and to remain operative as long as I wish it to. *Nothing* can get through it though I maintain it for as many years as I wish. Furthermore this building is now stocked with a tremendous quantity of supplies—of all kinds. Even chemicals and seeds for hydroponic gardens. There is enough of everything here to supply two people for—for their lifetimes."

"But—you're turning this over to the government, aren't you? If it's a defense against the H-bomb . . ."

Braden frowned. "It is, but unfortunately it turns out to have negligible, if any, military value. The high brass was right on that. You see, Myra, the power required to create such a force field varies with the cube of its size. The one about this building will be eighty feet in diameter—and when I turn it on the power drain will probably burn out the lighting system of Cleveland.

"To throw such a dome over—well, even over a tiny village or over a single military camp would take more electric power than is consumed by the whole country in weeks. And once turned off to let anything or anybody in or out it would require the same impracticable amount of power to recreate the field.

"The only conceivable use the government could make of it would be such use as I intend to make myself. To preserve the lives of one or two, at most a few individuals—to let them live through the holocaust and the savagery to come. And, except here, it's too late even for that."

"Too late—why?"

"There won't be time for them to construct the equipment. My dear, the war is on."

Her face grew white as she stared at him.

He said, "On the radio, a few minutes ago. Boston has been destroyed by an atomic bomb. War has been declared." He spoke faster. "And you know all that means and will lead to. I'm closing the switch that will put on the field and I'm keeping it on until it's safe to open it again." He didn't shock her further by saying that he didn't think it would be completely safe within their lifetimes. "We can't help anyone else now—it's too late. But we can save ourselves."

He sighed. "I'm sorry I had to be so abrupt about this. But now you understand why. In fact, I don't ask you to marry me right away, if you have any doubt at all. Just stay here until you're ready. Let me say the things, do the things, I should have said and done.

"Until now"—he smiled at her—"until now I've been working so hard, so many hours a day, that I haven't had time to make love to you. But now there'll *be* time, lots of time—and I *do* love you, Myra."

She stood up suddenly. Unseeingly, almost blindly, she started for the doorway.

"*Myra!*" he called. He started around the desk after her. She turned at the door and held him back. Her face and her voice were quite calm.

"I've got to go, Doctor. I've had a little nurse's training. I'm going to be needed."

"But, Myra, think what's going to happen out there! They're going to turn into animals. They're going to die horribly. Listen, I love you too much to let you face that. Stay, please!"

Amazingly she had smiled at him. "Good-bye, Dr. Braden. I'm afraid that I'm going to have to die with the rest of the animals. I guess I'm crazy that way."

And the door had closed behind her. From the window he had watched her go down the steps and start running as soon as she had reached the sidewalk.

There'd been the roar of jets overhead. Probably, he thought, this soon, they were ours. But they could be the enemy—over the pole and across Canada, so high that they'd escaped detection, swooping low as they crossed Erie. With Cleveland as one of their objectives. Maybe somehow they'd even know of him and his work and had made Cleveland a prime objective. He had run to the switch and thrown it.

Outside the window, twenty feet from it, a gray nothingness had sprung into being. All sound from outside had ceased. He had gone out of the house and looked at it— the visible half of it a gray hemisphere, forty feet high and eighty feet broad, just big enough to clear the two-story almost cubical building that was his home and his laboratory both. And he knew that it extended forty feet into the earth to complete a perfect sphere. No ravening force could enter it from above, no earthworm crawl through it from below.

None had for thirty years.

Well, it hadn't been too bad a thirty years, he thought. He'd had his books—and he'd read his favorite ones so often that he knew them almost by heart. He'd kept on experimenting and—although, the last seven years, since he'd passed sixty, he'd gradually lost interest and creativeness—he'd accomplished a few little things.

Nothing comparable to the field itself or even his inventions before that—but there hadn't been the incentive. Too slight a probability that anything he developed would ever be of use to himself or to anybody else. What good is a refinement in electronics to a savage who doesn't know how to tune a simple radio set, let alone build one.

Well, there'd been enough to keep him sane if not happy.

He went to the window and stared through it at the gray impalpability twenty feet away. If only he could lower it and then, when he saw what he knew he would see, restore it quickly. But once down it was down for good.

He walked to the switch and stood staring at it. Suddenly he reached up and pulled it. He turned slowly to the window and then walked, almost ran, to it. The gray wall was gone—what lay beyond it was sheerly incredible.

Not the Cleveland he'd known but a beautiful city, a *new* city. What had been a narrow street was a wide boulevard. The houses, the buildings, were clean and beautiful, the style of architecture strange to him. Grass, trees, everything well kept. What had happened—how could it be? After atomic war mankind couldn't possibly have come back this far, this quickly. Else all of sociology was wrong and ridiculous.

And where were the people? As if in answer a car went by. A car? It looked like no car he'd ever seen before. Much faster, much sleeker, much more maneuverable—it barely seemed to touch the street, as though anti-gravity took away its weight while gyroscopes gave it stability. A man and woman rode in it, the man driving. He was young and handsome, the woman young and beautiful.

They turned and looked his way and suddenly the man stopped the vehicle—stopped it in an incredibly short distance for the speed at which they'd been traveling. Of course, Braden thought—they've driven past here before and the gray dome was here and now it's gone. The car started up again. Braden thought, they've gone to tell someone.

He went to the door and outside, out onto the lovely boulevard. Out in the open he realized why there were so few people, so little traffic. His chronometers *had* gone wrong. Over thirty years they were off by hours at least. It was early morning—from the position of the Sun between six and seven o'clock.

He started walking. If he stayed there, in the house that had been thirty years under the dome, someone would come as soon as the young couple who had seen had reported. And yes, whoever came would explain what had happened but he wanted to figure it out for himself, to realize it more gradually than that.

He walked. He met no one. This was a fine residential part of town now and it was very early. He saw a few people at a distance. Their dress was different from his but not enough so as to make him an object of immediate curiosity. He saw more of the incredible vehicles but none of their occupants chanced to notice him. They traveled incredibly fast.

At last he came to a store that was open. He walked in, too consumed by excited curiosity by now to wait any longer. A young man with curly hair was arranging things behind the counter. He looked at Braden almost incredulously, then asked politely, "What can I do for you, sir?"

"Please don't think I'm crazy. I'll explain later. Just answer this. What happened thirty years ago? Wasn't there atomic war?"

The young man's eyes lighted. "Why, you must be the man who's been under the dome, sir. That explains why you . . ." He stopped as though embarrassed.

"Yes," Braden said. "I've been under the dome. But *what happened?* After Boston was destroyed what happened?"

"Space-ships, sir. The destruction of Boston was accidental. A fleet of ships came from Aldebaran. A race far more advanced than we and benevolent. They came to welcome us into the Union and to help us. Unfortunately one crashed—into Boston—and the atomics that powered it exploded, and a million were killed. But other ships landed everywhere within hours and explained and apologized and war was averted—very narrowly. United States air fleets were already en route, but they managed to call them back."

Braden said hoarsely, "Then there *was* no war?"

"Of course not. War is something back in the dark ages now, thanks to the Galactic Union. We haven't even national governments now to declare a war. There *can't* be war. And our progress, with the help of the Union, has been—well, tremendous. We've colonized Mars and Venus —they weren't inhabited and the Union assigned them to us so we could expand. But Mars and Venus are just suburbs. We travel to the stars. We've even . . ." He paused.

Braden held tightly to the edge of the counter. He'd missed it all. He'd been thirty years alone and now he was an old man. He asked, "You've even—what?" Something inside him told him what was coming and he could hardly hear his own voice.

"Well, we're not immortal but we're closer to it than

we were. We live for centuries. I wasn't much younger than you were thirty years ago. But—I'm afraid you missed out on it, sir. The processes the Union gave us work only on humans up to middle age—fifty at the very most. And you're—"

"Sixty-seven," Braden said stiffly. "Thank you."

Yes, he'd missed everything. The stars—he'd have given almost anything to go there but he didn't want to now. And Myra.

He could have had her and they'd both still be young.

He walked out of the store and turned his footsteps toward the building that had been under the dome. By now they'd be waiting for him there. And maybe they'd give him the only thing he'd ask of them—power to restore the force field so he could finish what was left of his life there under the dome. Yes, the only thing he wanted now was what he'd thought he wanted least—to die, as he had lived, alone.

BLOOD

IN THEIR TIME MACHINE, Vron and Dreena, last two survivors of the race of vampires, fled into the future to escape annihilation. They held hands and consoled one another in their terror and their hunger.

In the twenty-second century mankind had found them out, had discovered that the legend of vampires living secretly among humans was not a legend at all, but fact. There had been a pogrom that had found and killed every vampire but these two, who had already been working on a time machine and who had finished in time to escape in it. Into the future, far enough into the future that the very word *vampire* would be forgotten so they could again live unsuspected—and from their loins regenerate their race.

"I'm hungry, Vron. Awfully hungry."

"I too, Dreena dear. We'll stop again soon."

They had stopped four times already and had narrowly escaped dying each time. They had *not* been forgotten. The last stop, half a million years back, had shown them a world gone to the dogs—quite literally: human beings were extinct and dogs had become civilized and man-like. Still they had been recognized for what they were. They'd managed to feed once, on the blood of a tender young bitch, but then they'd been hounded back to their time machine and into flight again.

"Thanks for stopping," Dreena said. She sighed.

"Don't thank me," said Vron grimly. "This is the end of the line. We're out of fuel and we'll find none here—by now all radioactives will have turned to lead. We live here . . . or else."

They went out to scout. "Look," said Dreena excitedly,

pointing to something walking toward them. "A new creature! The dogs are gone and something else has taken over. And surely we're forgotten."

The approaching creature was telepathic. "I have heard your thoughts," said a voice inside their brains. "You wonder whether we know 'vampires,' whatever they are. We do not."

Dreena clutched Vron's arm in ecstasy. "Freedom!" she murmured hungrily. "And *food!*"

"You also wonder," said the voice, "about my origin and evolution. All life today is vegetable. I—" He bowed low to them. "I, a member of the dominant race, was once what you called a turnip."

HALL OF MIRRORS

FOR AN INSTANT you think it is temporary blindness, this sudden dark that comes in the middle of a bright afternoon.

It *must* be blindness, you think; could the sun that was tanning you have gone out instantaneously, leaving you in utter blackness?

Then the nerves of your body tell you that you are *standing,* whereas only a second ago you were sitting comfortably, almost reclining, in a canvas chair. In the patio of a friend's house in Beverly Hills. Talking to Barbara, your fiancée. Looking at Barbara—Barbara in a swim suit —her skin golden tan in the brilliant sunshine, beautiful.

You wore swimming trunks. Now you do not feel them on you; the slight pressure of the elastic waistband is no longer there against your waist. You touch your hands to your hips. You are naked. And standing.

Whatever has happened to you is more than a change to sudden darkness or to sudden blindness.

You raise your hands gropingly before you. They touch a plain smooth surface, a wall. You spread them apart and each hand reaches a corner. You pivot slowly. A second wall, then a third, then a door. You are in a closet about four feet square.

Your hand finds the knob of the door. It turns and you push the door open.

There is light now. The door has opened to a lighted room . . . a room that you have never seen before.

It is not large, but it is pleasantly furnished—although the furniture is of a style that is strange to you. Modesty makes you open the door cautiously the rest of the way. But the room is empty of people.

You step into the room, turning to look behind you into the closet, which is now illuminated by light from the room. The closet is and is not a closet; it is the size and shape of one, but it contains nothing, not a single hook, no rod for hanging clothes, no shelf. It is an empty, blank-walled, four-by-four foot space.

You close the door to it and stand looking around the room. It is about twelve by sixteen feet. There is one door, but it is closed. There are no windows. Five pieces of furniture. Four of them you recognize—more or less. One looks like a very functional desk. One is obviously a chair . . . a comfortable-looking one. There is a table, although its top is on several levels instead of only one. Another is a bed, or couch. Something shimmering is lying across it and you walk over and pick the shimmering something up and examine it. It is a garment.

You are naked, so you put it on. Slippers are part way under the bed (or couch) and you slide your feet into them. They fit, and they feel warm and comfortable as nothing you have ever worn on your feet has felt. Like lamb's wool, but softer.

You are dressed now. You look at the door—the only door of the room except that of the closet (closet?) from which you entered it. You walk to the door and before you try the knob, you see the small typewritten sign pasted just above it that reads:

This door has a time lock set to open in one hour. For reasons you will soon understand, it is better that you do not leave this room before then. There is a letter for you on the desk. Please read it.

It is not signed. You look at the desk and see that there is an envelope lying on it.

You do not yet go to take that envelope from the desk and read the letter that must be in it.

Why not? Because you are frightened.

You see other things about the room. The lighting has no source that you can discover. It comes from nowhere. It is not indirect lighting; the ceiling and the walls are not reflecting it at all.

They didn't have lighting like that, back where you came

from. What did you mean by *back where you came from?*

You close your eyes. You tell yourself: *I am Norman Hastings. I am an associate professor of mathematics at the University of Southern California. I am twenty-five years old, and this is the year nineteen hundred and fifty-four.*

You open your eyes and look again.

They didn't use that style of furniture in Los Angeles— or anywhere else that you know of—in 1954. That thing over in the corner—you can't even guess what it is. So might your grandfather, at your age, have looked at a television set.

You look down at yourself, at the shimmering garment that you found waiting for you. With thumb and forefinger you feel its texture.

It's like nothing you've ever touched before.

I am Norman Hastings. This is nineteen hundred and fifty-four.

Suddenly you must know, and at once.

You go to the desk and pick up the envelope that lies upon it. Your name is typed on the outside. *Norman Hastings.*

Your hands shake a little as you open it. Do you blame them?

There are several pages, typewritten. Dear Norman, it starts. You turn quickly to the end to look for the signature. It is unsigned.

You turn back and start reading.

"Do not be afraid. There is nothing to fear, but much to explain. Much that you must understand before the time lock opens that door. Much that you must accept and— obey.

"You have already guessed that you are in the future— in what, to you, seems to be the future. The clothes and the room must have told you that. I planned it that way so the shock would not be too sudden, so you would realize it over the course of several minutes rather than read it here—and quite probably disbelieve what you read.

"The 'closet' from which you have just stepped is, as you have by now realized, a time machine. From it you stepped into the world of 2004. The date is April 7th, just fifty years from the time you last remember.

"You cannot return.

"I did this to you and you may hate me for it; I do not know. That is up to you to decide, but it does not matter. What does matter, and not to you alone, is another decision which you must make. I am incapable of making it.

"Who is writing this to you? I would rather not tell you just yet. By the time you have finished reading this, even though it is not signed (for I knew you would look first for a signature), I will not need to tell you who I am. You will know.

"I am seventy-five years of age. I have, in this year 2004, been studying 'time' for thirty of those years. I have completed the first time machine ever built—and thus far, its construction, even the fact that it has been constructed, is my own secret.

"You have just participated in the first major experiment. It will be your responsibility to decide whether there shall ever be any more experiments with it, whether it should be given to the world, or whether it should be destroyed and never used again."

End of the first page. You look up for a moment, hesitating to turn the next page. Already you suspect what is coming.

You turn the page.

"I constructed the first time machine a week ago. My calculations had told me that it would work, but not how it would work. I had expected it to send an object back in time—it works backward in time only, not forward—physically unchanged and intact.

"My first experiment showed me my error. I placed a cube of metal in the machine—it was a miniature of the one you just walked out of—and set the machine to go backward ten years. I flicked the switch and opened the door, expecting to find the cube vanished. Instead I found it had crumbled to powder.

"I put in another cube and sent it two years back. The second cube came back unchanged, except that it was newer, shinier.

"That gave me the answer. I had been expecting the cubes to go back in time, and they had done so, but not in the sense I had expected them to. Those metal cubes had been fabricated about three years previously. I had sent the first one back years before it had existed in its fabricated form. Ten years ago it had been ore. The machine returned it to that state.

"Do you see how our previous theories of time travel have been wrong? We expected to be able to step into a time machine in, say, 2004, set it for fifty years back, and then step out in the year 1954 . . . but it does not work that way. The machine does not move in time. Only whatever is within the machine is affected, and then just with relation to itself and not to the rest of the Universe.

"I confirmed this with guinea pigs by sending one six weeks old five weeks back and it came out a baby.

"I need not outline all my experiments here. You will find a record of them in the desk and you can study it later.

"Do you understand now what has happened to you, Norman?"

You begin to understand. And you begin to sweat.

The *I* who wrote that letter you are now reading is *you,* yourself at the age of seventy-five, in the year of 2004. You are that seventy-five-year-old man, with your body returned to what it had been fifty years ago, with all the memories of fifty years of living wiped out.

You invented the time machine.

And before you used it on yourself, you made these arrangements to help you orient yourself. You wrote yourself the letter which you are now reading.

But if those fifty years are—to you—gone, what of all your friends, those you loved? What of your parents? What of the girl you are going—were going—to marry?

You read on:

"Yes, you will want to know what has happened. Mom died in 1963, Dad in 1968. You married Barbara in 1956. I am sorry to tell you that she died only three years later, in a plane crash. You have one son. He is still living; his name is Walter; he is now forty-six years old and is an accountant in Kansas City."

Tears come into your eyes and for a moment you can no longer read. Barbara dead—dead for forty-five years. And only minutes ago, in subjective time, you were sitting next to her, sitting in the bright sun in a Beverly Hills patio . . .

You force yourself to read again.

"But back to the discovery. You begin to see some of its implications. You will need time to think to see all of them.

"It does not permit time travel as we have thought of time travel, but it gives us immortality of a sort. Immortality of the kind I have temporarily given us.

"*Is it good?* Is it worth while to lose the memory of fifty years of one's life in order to return one's body to relative youth? The only way I can find out is to try, as soon as I have finished writing this and made my other preparations.

"You will know the answer.

"But before you decide, remember that there is another problem, more important than the psychological one. I mean overpopulation.

"If our discovery is given to the world, if all who are old or dying can make themselves young again, the population will almost double every generation. Nor would the world—not even our own relatively enlightened country—be willing to accept compulsory birth control as a solution.

"Give this to the world, as the world is today in 2004, and within a generation there will be famine, suffering, war. Perhaps a complete collapse of civilization.

"Yes, we have reached other planets, but they are not suitable for colonizing. The stars may be our answer, but we are a long way from reaching them. When we do, someday, the billions of habitable planets that must be out there will be our answer . . . our living room. But until then, what is the answer?

"Destroy the machine? But think of the countless lives it can save, the suffering it can prevent. Think of what it would mean to a man dying of cancer. Think . . ."

Think. You finish the letter and put it down.

You think of Barbara dead for forty-five years. And of the fact that you were married to her for three years and that those years are lost to you.

Fifty years lost. You damn the old man of seventy-five whom you became and who has done this to you . . . who has given you this decision to make.

Bitterly, you know what the decision must be. You think

that *he* knew, too, and realize that he could safely leave it in your hands. Damn him, he *should* have known.

Too valuable to destroy, too dangerous to give.

The other answer is painfully obvious.

You must be custodian of this discovery and keep it secret until it is safe to give, until mankind has expanded to the stars and has new worlds to populate, or until, even without that, he has reached a state of civilization where he can avoid overpopulaion by rationing births to the number of accidental—or voluntary—deaths.

If neither of those things has happened in another fifty years (and are they likely so soon?), then you, at seventy-five, will by writing another letter like this one. You will be undergoing another experience similar to the one you're going through now. And making the same decision, of course.

Why not? You'll be the same person again.

Time and again, to preserve this secret until Man is ready for it.

How often will you again sit at a desk like this one, thinking the thoughts you are thinking now, feeling the grief you now feel?

There is a click at the door and you know that the time lock has opened, that you are now free to leave this room, free to start a new life for yourself in place of the one you have already lived and lost.

But you are in no hurry now to walk directly through that door.

You sit there, staring straight ahead of you blindly, seeing in your mind's eye the vista of a set of facing mirrors, like those in an old-fashioned barber shop, reflecting the same thing over and over again, diminishing into far distance.

EXPERIMENT

"**T**HE FIRST time machine, gentlemen," Professor Johnson proudly informed his two colleagues. "True, it is a small-scale experimental model. It will operate only on objects weighing less than three pounds, five ounces and for distances into the past and future of twelve minutes or less. But it works."

The small-scale model looked like a small scale—a postage scale—except for two dials in the part under the platform.

Professor Johnson held up a small metal cube. "Our experimental object," he said, "is a brass cube weighing one pound, two point, three ounces. First, I shall send it five minutes into the future."

He leaned forward and set one of the dials on the time machine. "Look at your watches," he said.

They looked at their watches. Professor Johnson placed the cube gently on the machine's platform. It vanished.

Five minutes later, to the second, it reappeared.

Professor Johnson picked it up. "Now five minutes into the past." He set the other dial. Holding the cube in his hand he looked at his watch. "It is six minutes before three o'clock. I shall now activate the mechanism—by placing the cube on the platform—at exactly three o'clock. Therefore, the cube should, at five minutes before three, vanish from my hand and appear on the platform, five minutes before I place it there."

"How can you place it there, then?" asked one of his colleagues.

"It will, as my hand approaches, vanish from the platform and appear in my hand to be placed there. Three o'clock. Notice, please."

The cube vanished from his hand.

It appeared on the platform of the time machine.

"See? Five minutes before I shall place it there, it *is* there!"

His other colleague frowned at the cube. "But," he said, "what if, now that it has already appeared five minutes before you place it there, you should change your mind about doing so and *not* place it there at three o'clock? Wouldn't there be a paradox of some sort involved?"

"An interesting idea," Professor Johnson said. "I had not thought of it, and it will be interesting to try. Very well, I shall *not* . . ."

There was no paradox at all. The cube remained.

But the entire rest of the Universe, professors and all, vanished.

THE LAST MARTIAN

IT WAS an evening like any evening, but duller than most. I was back in the city room after covering a boring banquet, at which the food had been so poor that, even though it had cost me nothing, I'd felt cheated. For the hell of it, I was writing a long and glowing account of it, ten or twelve column inches. The copyreader, of course, would cut it to a passionless paragraph or two.

Slepper was sitting with his feet up on the desk, ostentatiously doing nothing, and Johnny Hale was putting a new ribbon on his typewriter. The rest of the boys were out on routine assignments.

Cargan, the city ed, came out of his private office and walked over to us.

"Any of you guys know Barney Welch?" he asked us.

A silly question. Barney runs Barney's Bar right across the street from the Trib. There isn't a Trib reporter who doesn't know Barney well enough to borrow money from him. So we all nodded.

"He just phoned," Cargan said. "He's got a guy down there who claims to be from Mars."

"Drunk or crazy, which?" Slepper wanted to know.

"Barney doesn't know, but he said there might be a gag story in it if we want to come over and talk to the guy. Since it's right across the street and since you three mugs are just sitting on your prats, anyway, one of you dash over. But no drinks on the expense account."

Slepper said, "I'll go," but Cargan's eyes had lighted on me. "You free, Bill?" he asked. "This has got to be a funny story, if any, and you got a light touch on the human interest stuff."

"Sure," I grumbled. "I'll go."

"Maybe it's just some drunk being funny, but if the guy's really insane, phone for a cop, unless you think you can get a gag story. If there's an arrest, you got something to hang a straight story on."

Slepper said, "Cargan, you'd get your grandmother arrested to get a story. Can I go along with Bill, just for the ride?"

"No, you and Johnny stay here. We're not moving the city room across the street to Barney's." Cargan went back into his office.

I slapped a "thirty" on to end the banquet story and sent it down the tube. I got my hat and coat. Slepper said, "Have a drink for me, Bill. But don't drink so much you lose that light touch."

I said, "Sure," and went on over to the stairway and down.

I walked into Barney's and looked around. Nobody from the Trib was there except a couple of pressmen playing gin rummy at one of the tables. Aside from Barney himself, back of the bar, there was only one other man in the place. He was a tall man, thin and sallow, who was sitting by himself in one of the booths, staring morosely into an almost empty beer glass.

I thought I'd get Barney's angle first, so I went up to the bar and put down a bill. "A quick one," I told him. "Straight, water on the side. And is tall-and-dismal over there the Martian you phoned Cargan about?"

He nodded once and poured my drink.

"What's my angle?" I asked him. "Does he know a reporter's going to interview him? Or do I just buy him a drink and rope him, or what? How crazy is he?"

"You tell me. Says he just got in from Mars two hours ago and he's trying to figure it out. He says he's the last living Martian. He doesn't know you're a reporter, but he's all set to talk to you. I set it up."

"How?"

"Told him I had a friend who was smarter than any usual guy and could give him good advice on what to do. I didn't tell him any name because I didn't know who Cargan would send. But he's all ready to cry on your shoulder."

"Know *his* name?"

Barney grimaced. "Yangan Dal, he says. Listen, don't get him violent or anything in here. I don't want no trouble."

I downed my shot and took a sip of chaser. I said, "Okay, Barney. Look, dish up two beers for us and I'll go over and take 'em with me."

Barney drew two beers and cut off their heads. He rang up sixty cents and gave me my change, and I went over to the booth with the beers.

"Mr. Dal?" I said. "My name is Bill Everett. Barney tells me you have a problem I might help you on."

He looked up at me. "You're the one he phoned? Sit down, Mr. Everett. And thanks very much for the beer."

I slid into the booth across from him. He took the last sip of his previous beer and wrapped nervous hands around the glass I'd just bought him.

"I suppose you'll think I'm crazy," he said. "And maybe you'll be right, but—I don't understand it myself. The bartender thinks I'm crazy, I guess. Listen, are you a doctor?"

"Not exactly," I told him. "Call me a consulting psychologist."

"Do you think I'm insane?"

I said, "Most people who are don't admit they might be. But I haven't heard your story yet."

He took a draught of the beer and put the glass down again, but kept his hands tightly around the glass, possibly to keep them from shaking.

He said, "I'm a Martian. *The last one.* All the others are dead. I saw their bodies only two hours ago."

"You were on Mars only two hours ago? How did you get here?"

"I don't know. That's the horrible thing. I don't know. All I know is that the others were dead, their bodies starting to rot. It was awful. There were a hundred million of us, and now I'm the last one."

"A hundred million. That's the population of Mars?"

"About that. A little over, maybe. But that *was* the population. They're all dead now, except me. I looked in three cities, the three biggest ones. I was in Skar, and when

I found all the people dead there, I took a targan—there was no one to stop me—and flew it to Undanel. I'd never flown one before, but the controls were simple. Everyone in Undanel was dead, too. I refueled and flew on. I flew low and watched and there was no one alive. I flew to Zandar, the biggest city—over three million people. And all of them were dead and starting to rot. It was horrible, I tell you. Horrible. I can't get over the shock of it."

"I can imagine," I said.

"You *can't*. Of course it was a dying world, anyway; we didn't have more than another dozen generations left to us, you understand. Two centuries ago, we numbered three billion—most of them starving. It was the kryl, the disease that came from the desert wind and that our scientists couldn't cure. In two centuries it reduced us to one-thirtieth of our number and it still kept on."

"Your people died, then, of this—kryl?"

"No. When a Martian dies of kryl, he withers. The corpses I saw were not withered." He shuddered and drank the rest of his beer. I saw that I'd neglected mine and downed it. I raised two fingers at Barney, who was watching our way and looking worried.

My Martian went on talking. "We tried to develop space travel, but we couldn't. We thought some of us might escape the kryl, if we came to Earth or to other worlds. We tried, but we failed. We couldn't even get to Deimos or Phobos, our moons."

"You didn't develop space travel? Then how—"

"I don't know. *I don't know,* and I tell you it's driving me wild. I don't know how I got here. I'm Yangan Dal, *a Martian. And I'm here, in this body.* It's driving me wild, I tell you."

Barney came with the beers. He looked worried enough, so I waited until he was out of hearing before I asked, "In this body? Do you mean—"

"Of course. This isn't *I,* this body I'm in. You don't think Martians would look exactly like humans, do you? I'm three feet tall, weigh what would be about twenty pounds here on Earth. I have four arms with six-fingered hands. This body I'm in—it frightens me. I don't understand it, any more than I know how I got here."

"Or how you happen to talk English? Or can you account for that?"

"Well—in a way I can. This body; its name is Howard Wilcox. It's a bookkeeper. It's married to a female of this species. It works at a place called the Humbert Lamp Company. I've got all its memories and I can do everything it could do; I know everything it knew, or knows. In a sense, I *am* Howard Wilcox. I've got stuff in my pockets to prove it. But it doesn't make sense, because I'm Yangan Dal, and I'm a Martian. I've even got this body's tastes. I like beer. And if I think about this body's wife, I—well, I love her."

I stared at him and pulled out my cigarettes, held out the package to him. "Smoke?"

"This body—Howard Wilcox—doesn't smoke. Thanks, though. And let me buy us another round of beers. There's money in these pockets."

I signaled Barney.

"When did this happen? You say only two hours ago? Did you ever suspect before then that you were a Martian?"

"Suspect? I *was* a Martian. What time is it?"

I looked at Barney's clock. "A little after nine."

"Then it's a little longer than I thought. Three and a half hours. It would have been half past five when I found myself in this body, because it was going home from work then, and from its memories I know it had left work half an hour before then, at five."

"And did you—it—go home?"

"No, I was too confused. It wasn't *my* home. I'm a *Martian*. Don't you understand that? Well, I don't blame you if you don't, because I don't, either. But I walked. And I—I mean Howard Wilcox—got thirsty and he—I—" He stopped and started over again. "This body got thirsty and I stopped in here for a drink. After two or three beers, I thought maybe the bartender there could give me some advice and I started talking to him."

I leaned forward across the table. "Listen, Howard," I said, "you were due home for dinner. You're making your wife worry like anything about you unless you phoned her. Did you?"

"Did I— Of course not. I'm not Howard Wilcox." But a new type of worry came into his face.

"You'd better phone her," I said. "What's there to lose? Whether you are Yangan Dal or Howard Wilcox, there's a woman sitting home worrying about you or him. Be kind enough to phone her. Do you know the number?"

"Of course. It's my own—I mean it's Howard Wilcox's—"

"Quit tying yourself into grammatical knots and go make that phone call. Don't worry about thinking up a story yet; you're too confused. Just tell her you'll explain when you get home, but that you're all right."

He got up like a man in a daze and headed for the phone booth.

I went over to the bar and had another quickie, straight. Barney said, "Is he—uh—"

"I don't know yet," I said. "There's something about it I still don't get."

I got back to the booth.

He was grinning weakly. He said, "She sounded madder than hoptoads. If I—if Howard Wilcox does go home, his story had better be good." He took a gulp of beer. "Better than Yangan Dal's story, anyway." He was getting more human by the moment.

But then he was back into it again. He stared at me. "I maybe should have told you how it happened from the beginning. I was shut up in a room on Mars. In the city of Skar. I don't know why they put me there, but they did. I was locked in. And then for a long time they didn't bring me food, and I got so hungry that I worked a stone loose from the floor and started to scrape my way through the door. I was starving. It took me three days—Martian days, about six Earth days—to get through, and I staggered around until I found the food quarters of the building I was in. There was no one there and I ate. And then—"

"Go on," I said. "I'm listening."

"I went out of the building and everyone was lying in the open, in the streets, dead. Rotting." He put his hands over his eyes. "I looked in some houses, other buildings. I don't know why or what I was looking for, but nobody had died indoors. Everybody was lying dead in the open, and none of the bodies were withered, so it wasn't kryl that killed them.

"Then, as I told you, I stole the targan—or I guess I

really didn't steal it, because there was no one to steal it from—and flew around looking for someone alive. Out in the country it was the same way—everybody lying in the open, near the houses, dead. And Undanel and Zandar, the same.

"Did I tell you Zandar's the biggest city, the capital? In the middle of Zandar there's a big open space, the Games Field, that's more than an Earth-mile square. And all the people in Zandar were there, or it looked like all. Three million bodies, all lying together, like they'd gathered there to die, out in the open. Like they'd known. Like everyone, everywhere else, was out in the open, but here they were all together, the whole three million of them.

"I saw it from the air, as I flew over the city. And there was something in the middle of the field, on a platform. I went down and hovered the targan—it's a little like your helicopters, I forgot to mention—I hovered over the platform to see what was there. It was some kind of a column made of solid copper. Copper on Mars is like gold is on Earth. There was a push-button set with precious stones set in the column. And a Martian in a blue robe lay dead at the foot of the column, right under the button. As though he'd pushed it—and then died. And everybody else had died, too, with him. Everybody on Mars, except me.

"And I lowered the targan onto the platform and got out and I pushed the button. I wanted to die, too; everybody else was dead and I wanted to die, too. *But I didn't. I was riding on a streetcar on Earth, on my way home from work, and my name was—*"

I signaled Barney.

"Listen, Howard," I said. "We'll have one more beer and then you'd better get home to your wife. You'll catch hell from her, even now, and the longer you wait, the worse it'll be. And if you're smart, you'll take some candy or flowers along and think up a really good story on the way home. And *not* the one you just told me."

He said, "Well—"

I said, "Well me no wells. Your name is Howard Wilcox and you'd better get home to your wife. I'll tell you what *may* have happened. We know little about the human mind, and many strange things happen to it. Maybe the medieval people *had* something when they believed in possession. Do you want to know what I think happened to you?"

"What? For Heaven's sake, if you can give me *any* explanation—except tell me that I'm crazy—"

"I think you *can* drive yourself batty if you let yourself think about it, Howard. Assume there's some natural explanation and then forget it. I can make a random guess what may have happened."

Barney came with the beers and I waited until he'd gone back to the bar.

I said, "Howard, just possibly a man—I mean a Martian —named Yangan Dal did die this afternoon on Mars. Maybe he really was the last Martian. And maybe, somehow, his mind got mixed up with yours at the moment of his death. I'm not saying that's what happened, but it isn't impossible to believe. Assume it was that, Howard, and fight it off. Just act as though you are Howard Wilcox— and look in a mirror if you doubt it. Go home and square things with your wife, and then go to work tomorrow morning and forget it. Don't you think that's the best idea?"

"Well, maybe you're right. The evidence of my senses—"

"Accept it. Until and unless you get better evidence."

We finished off our beers and I put him into a taxi. I reminded him to stop for candy or flowers and to work up a good and reasonable alibi, instead of thinking about what he'd been telling me.

I went back upstairs in the Trib building and into Cargan's office and closed the door behind me.

I said, "It's all right, Cargan. I straightened him out."

"What had happened?"

"He's a Martian, all right. And he was the last Martian left on Mars. Only he didn't know we'd come here; he thought we were all dead."

"But how— How could he have been overlooked? How could he not have known?"

I said, "He's an imbecile. He was in a mental institution in Skar and somebody slipped up and left him in his room when the button was pushed that sent us here. He wasn't out in the open, so he didn't get the mentaport rays that carried our psyches across space. He escaped from his room and found the platform in Zandar, where the ceremony was, and pushed the button himself. There must have been enough juice left to send him after us."

Cargan whistled softly. "Did you tell him the truth? And is he smart enough to keep his trap shut?"

I shook my head. "No, to both questions. His I. Q. is about fifteen, at a guess. But that's as smart as the average Earthman, so he'll get by here all right. I convinced him he really was the Earthman his psyche happened to get into."

"Lucky thing he went into Barney's. I'll phone Barney in a minute and let him know it's taken care of. I'm surprised he didn't give the guy a mickey before he phoned us."

I said, "Barney's one of us. He wouldn't have let the guy get out of there. He'd have held him till we got there."

"But you let him go. Are you sure it's safe? Shouldn't you have—"

"He'll be all right," I said. "I'll assume responsibility to keep an eye on him until we take over. I suppose we'll have to instutionalize him again after that. But I'm glad I didn't have to kill him. After all, he *is* one of us, imbecile or not. And he'll probably be so glad to learn he isn't the *last* Martian that he won't mind having to return to an asylum."

I went back into the city room and to my desk. Slepper was gone, sent out somewhere on something. Johnny Hale looked up from the magazine he was reading. "Get a story?" he asked.

"Nah," I said. "Just a drunk being the life of the party. I'm surprised at Barney for calling."

SENTRY

H E WAS WET and muddy and hungry and cold and he was fifty thousand light-years from home.

A strange blue sun gave light and the gravity, twice what he was used to, made every movement difficult.

But in tens of thousands of years this part of war hadn't changed. The flyboys were fine with their sleek spaceships and their fancy weapons. When the chips are down, though, it was still the foot soldier, the infantry, that had to take the ground and hold it, foot by bloody foot. Like this damned planet of a star he'd never heard of until they'd landed him there. And now it was sacred ground because the aliens were there too. *The* aliens, the only other intelligent race in the Galaxy . . . cruel, hideous and repulsive monsters.

Contact had been made with them near the center of the Galaxy, after the slow, difficult colonization of a dozen thousand planets; and it had been war at sight; they'd shot without even trying to negotiate, or to make peace.

Now, planet by bitter planet, it was being fought out.

He was wet and muddy and hungry and cold, and the day was raw with a high wind that hurt his eyes. But the aliens were trying to infiltrate and every sentry post was vital.

He stayed alert, gun ready. Fifty thousand light-years from home, fighting on a strange world and wondering if he'd ever live to see home again.

And then he saw one of them crawling toward him. He drew a bead and fired. The alien made that strange horrible sound they all make, then lay still.

He shuddered at the sound and sight of the alien lying

there. One ought to be able to get used to them after a while, but he'd never been able to. Such repulsive creatures they were, with only two arms and two legs, ghastly white skins and no scales.

MOUSE

Bill Wheeler was, as it happened, looking out of the window of his bachelor apartment on the fifth floor on the corner of 83rd Street and Central Park West when the spaceship from Somewhere landed.

It floated gently down out of the sky and came to rest in Central Park on the open grass between the Simon Bolivar Monument and the walk, barely a hundred yards from Bill Wheeler's window.

Bill Wheeler's hand paused in stroking the soft fur of the Siamese cat lying on the windowsill and he said wonderingly, "What's that, Beautiful?" but the Siamese cat didn't answer. She stopped purring, though, when Bill stopped stroking her. She must have felt something different in Bill—possibly from the sudden rigidness in his fingers or possibly because cats are prescient and feel changes of mood. Anyway she rolled over on her back and said, "Miaouw," quite plaintively. But Bill, for once, didn't answer her. He was too engrossed in the incredible thing across the street in the park.

It was cigar-shaped, about seven feet long and two feet in diameter at the thickest point. As far as size was concerned, it might have been a large toy model dirigible, but it never occurred to Bill—even at his first glimpse of it when it was about fifty feet in the air, just opposite his window—that it might be a toy or a model.

There was something about it, even at the most casual look, that said *alien*. You couldn't put your finger on what it was. Anyway, alien or terrestrial, it had no visible means of support. No wings, propellers, rocket tubes or anything else—and it was made of metal and obviously heavier than air.

But it floated down like a feather to a point just about a foot above the grass. It stopped there and suddenly, out of one end of it (both ends were so nearly alike that you couldn't say it was the front or back) came a flash of fire that was almost blinding. There was a hissing sound with the flash and the cat under Bill Wheeler's hand turned over and was on her feet in a single lithe movement, looking out of the window. She spat once, softly, and the hairs on her back and the back of her neck stood straight up, as did her tail, which was now a full two inches thick.

Bill didn't touch her; if you know cats you don't when they're like that. But he said, "Quiet, Beautiful. It's all right. It's only a spaceship from Mars, to conquer Earth. It isn't a mouse."

He was right on the first count, in a way. He was wrong on the second, in a way. But let's not get ahead of ourselves like that.

After the single blast from its exhaust tube or whatever it was the spaceship dropped the last twelve inches and lay inert on the grass. It didn't move. There was now a fan-shaped area of blackened earth radiating from one end of it, for a distance of about thirty feet.

And then nothing happened except that people came running from several directions. Cops came running, too, three of them, and kept people from going too close to the alien object. Too close, according to the cops' idea, seemed to be closer than about ten feet. Which, Bill Wheeler thought, was silly. If the thing was going to explode or anything, it would probably kill everyone for blocks around.

But it didn't explode. It just lay there, and nothing happened. Nothing except that flash that had startled both Bill and the cat. And the cat looked bored now, and lay back down on the windowsill, her hackles down.

Bill stroked her sleek fawn-colored fur again, absent-mindedly. He said, "This is a day, Beautiful. That thing out there is from *outside,* or I'm a spider's nephew. I'm going down and take a look at it."

He took the elevator down. He got as far as the front door, tried to open it, and couldn't. All he could see through the glass was the backs of people, jammed tight against the door. Standing on tiptoes and stretching his neck to see over the nearest ones, he could see a solid phalanx of heads stretching from here to there.

He got back in the elevator. The operator said, "Sounds like excitement out front. Parade going by or something?"

"Something," Bill said. "Spaceship just landed in Central Park, from Mars or somewhere. You hear the welcoming committee out there."

"The hell," said the operator. "What's it doing?"

"Nothing."

The operator grinned. "You're a great kidder, Mr. Wheeler. How's that cat you got?"

"Fine," said Bill. "How's yours?"

"Getting crankier. Threw a book at me when I got home last night with a few under my belt and lectured me half the night because I'd spent three and a half bucks. You got the best kind."

"I think so," Bill said.

By the time he got back to the window, there was really a crowd down there. Central Park West was solid with people for half a block each way and the park was solid with them for a long way back. The only open area was a circle around the spaceship, now expanded to about twenty feet in radius, and with a lot of cops keeping it open instead of only three.

Bill Wheeler gently moved the Siamese over to one side of the windowsill and sat down. He said, "We got a box seat, Beautiful. I should have had more sense than to go down there."

The cops below were having a tough time. But reinforcements were coming, truckloads of them. They fought their way into the circle and then helped enlarge it. Somebody had obviously decided that the larger that circle was the fewer people were going to be killed. A few khaki uniforms had infiltrated the circle, too.

"Brass," Bill told the cat. "High brass. I can't make out insignia from here, but that one boy's at least a three-star; you can tell by the way he walks."

They got the circle pushed back to the sidewalk, finally. There was a lot of brass inside by then. And half a dozen men, some in uniform, some not, were starting, very carefully, to work on the ship. Photographs first, and then measurements, and then one man with a big suitcase of paraphernalia was carefully scratching at the metal and making tests of some kind.

"A metallurgist, Beautiful," Bill Wheeler explained to the Siamese, who wasn't watching at all. "And I'll bet you ten pounds of liver to one miaouw he finds that's an alloy that's brand new to him. And that it's got some stuff in it he can't identify.

"You really ought to be looking out, Beautiful, instead of lying there like a dope. This is a *day*, Beautiful. This may be the beginning of the end—or of something new. I wish they'd hurry up and get it open."

Army trucks were coming into the circle now. Half a dozen big planes were circling overhead, making a lot of noise. Bill looked up at them quizzically.

"Bombers, I'll bet, with pay loads. Don't know what they have in mind unless to bomb the park, people and all, if little green men come out of that thing with ray guns and start killing everybody. Then the bombers could finish off whoever's left."

But no little green men came out of the cylinder. The men working on it couldn't, apparently, find an opening in it. They'd rolled it over now and exposed the under side, but the under side was the same as the top. For all they could tell, the under side *was* the top.

And then Bill Wheeler swore. The army trucks were being unloaded, and sections of a big tent were coming out of them, and men in khaki were driving stakes and unrolling canvas.

"They *would* do something like that, Beautiful," Bill complained bitterly. "Be bad enough if they hauled it off, but to leave it there to work on and still to block off our view—"

The tent went up. Bill Wheeler watched the top of the tent but nothing happened to the top of the tent and whatever went on inside he couldn't see. Trucks came and went, high brass and civvies came and went.

And after a while the phone rang. Bill gave a last affectionate rumple to the cat's fur and went to answer it.

"Bill Wheeler?" the receiver asked. "This is General Kelly speaking. Your name has been given to me as a competent research biologist. Tops in your field. Is that correct?"

"Well," Bill said. "I'm a research biologist. It would be hardly modest for me to say I'm tops in my field. What's up?"

"A spaceship has just landed in Central Park."

"You don't say," said Bill.

"I'm calling from the field of operations; we've run phones in here, and we're gathering specialists. We would like you and some other biologists to examine something that was found inside the—uh—spaceship. Grimm of Harvard was in town and will be here and Winslow of New York University is already here. It's opposite Eighty-third Street. How long would it take you to get here?"

"About ten seconds, if I had a parachute. I've been watching you out of my window." He gave the address and the apartment number. "If you can spare a couple of strong boys in imposing uniforms to get me through the crowd, it'll be quicker than if I try it myself. Okay?"

"Right. Send 'em right over. Sit tight."

"Good," said Bill. *"What* did you find inside the cylinder?"

There was a second's hesitation. Then the voice said, "Wait till you get here."

"I've got instruments," Bill said. "Dissecting equipment. Chemicals. Reagents. I want to know what to bring. Is it a little green man?"

"No," said the voice. After a second's hesitation again, it said, "It seems to be a mouse. A dead mouse."

"Thanks," said Bill. He put down the receiver and walked back to the window. He looked at the Siamese cat accusingly. "Beautiful," he demanded, "was somebody ribbing me, or—"

There was a puzzled frown on his face as he watched the scene across the street. Two policemen came hurrying out of the tent and headed directly for the entrance of his apartment building. They began to work their way through the crowd.

"Fan me with a blowtorch, Beautiful," Bill said. "It's the McCoy." He went to the closet and grabbed a valise, hurried to a cabinet and began to stuff instruments and bottles into the valise. He was ready by the time there was a knock on the door.

He said, "Hold the fort, Beautiful. Got to see a man about a mouse." He joined the policemen waiting outside his door and was escorted through the crowd and into the circle of the elect and into the tent.

There was a crowd around the spot where the cyclinder lay. Bill peered over shoulders and saw that the cylinder was neatly split in half. The inside was hollow and padded with something that looked like fine leather, but softer. A man kneeling at one end of it was talking.

"—not a trace of any activating mechanism, any mechanism at *all*, in fact. Not a wire, not a grain or a drop of any fuel. Just a hollow cylinder, padded inside. Gentlemen, it *couldn't* have traveled by its own power in any conceivable way. But it came here, and from outside. Gravesend says the material is definitely extra-terrestrial. Gentlemen, I'm stumped."

Another voice said, "I've an idea, Major." It was the voice of the man over whose shoulder Bill Wheeler was leaning and Bill recognized the voice and the man with a start. It was the President of the United States. Bill quit leaning on him.

"I'm no scientist," the President said. "And this is just a possibility. Remember the one blast, out of that single exhaust hole? That might have been the destruction, the dissipation of whatever the mechanism or the propellant was. Whoever, whatever, sent or guided this contraption might not have wanted us to find out what made it run. It was constructed, in that case, so that, upon landing, the mechanism destroyed itself utterly. Colonel Roberts, you examined that scorched area of ground. Anything that might bear out that theory?"

"Definitely, sir," said another voice. "Traces of metal and silica and some carbon, as though it had been vaporized by terrific heat and then condensed and uniformly spread. You can't find a chunk of it to pick up, but the instruments indicate it. Another thing—"

Someone was leaning over Bill's shoulder, putting un-Wheeler, aren't you?"

Bill turned. "Professor Winslow!" he said. "I've seen your picture, sir, and I've read your papers in the Journal. I'm proud to meet you and to—"

"Cut the malarkey," said Professor Winslow, "and take a gander at this." He grabbed Bill Wheeler by the arm and led him to a table in one corner of the tent.

"Looks for all the world like a dead mouse," he said, "but it isn't. Not quite. I haven't cut in yet; waited for you and Grimm. But I've taken temperature tests and had hairs under the mike and studied musculature. It's—well, look for yourself."

Bill Wheeler looked. It looked like a mouse all right, a very small mouse, until you looked closely. Then you saw little differences, if you were a biologist.

Grimm got there and—delicately, reverently—they cut in. The differences stopped being little ones and became big ones. The bones didn't seem to be made of bone, for one thing, and they were bright yellow instead of white. The digestive system wasn't too far off the beam, and there was a circulatory system and a white milky fluid in it, but there wasn't any heart. There were, instead, nodes at regular intervals along the larger tubes.

"Way stations," Grimm said. "No central pump. You might call it a lot of little hearts instead of one big one. Efficient, I'd say. Creature built like this couldn't have heart trouble. Here, let me put some of that white fluid on a slide."

Someone was leaning over Bill's shoulder, putting uncomfortable weight on him. He turned his head to tell the man to get the hell away and saw it was the President of the United States. "Out of this world?" the President asked quietly.

"And how," said Bill. A second later he added, "Sir," and the President chuckled. He asked, "Would you say it's been dead long or that it died about the time of arrival?"

Winslow answered that one. "It's purely a guess, Mr. President, because we don't know the chemical make-up of the thing, or what its normal temperature is. But a rectal thermometer reading twenty minutes ago, when I got here, was ninety-five three and one minute ago it was ninety point six. At that rate of heat loss, it couldn't have been dead long."

"Would you say it was an intelligent creature?"

"I wouldn't say for sure, Sir. It's too alien. But I'd guess

—definitely no. No more so than its terrestrial counterpart, a mouse. Brain size and convolutions are quite similar."

"You don't think it could, conceivably, have designed that ship?"

"I'd bet a million to one against it, Sir."

It had been mid-afternoon when the spaceship had landed; it was almost midnight when Bill Wheeler started home. Not from across the street, but from the lab at New York U., where the dissection and microscopic examinations had continued.

He walked home in a daze, but he remembered guiltily that the Siamese hadn't been fed, and hurried as much as he could for the last block.

She looked at him reproachfully and said "Miaouw, miaouw, miaouw, miaouw—" so fast he couldn't get a word in edgewise until she was eating some liver out of the icebox.

"Sorry, Beautiful," he said then. "Sorry, too, I couldn't bring you that mouse, but they wouldn't have let me if I'd asked, and I didn't ask because it would probably have given you indigestion."

He was still so excited that he couldn't sleep that night. When it got early enough he hurried out for the morning papers to see if there had been any new discoveries or developments.

There hadn't been. There was less in the papers than he knew already. But it was a big story and the papers played it big.

He spent most of three days at the New York U. lab, helping with further tests and examinations until there just weren't any new ones to try and darn little left to try them on. Then the government took over what was left and Bill Wheeler was on the outside again.

For three more days he stayed home, tuned in on all news reports on the radio and video and subscribed to every newspaper published in English in New York City. But the story gradually died down. Nothing further happened; no further discoveries were made and if any new ideas developed, they weren't given out for public consumption.

It was on the sixth day that an even bigger story broke —the assassination of the President of the United States. People forgot the spaceship.

Two days later the prime minister of Great Britain was killed by a Spaniard and the day after that a minor employe of the Politburo in Moscow ran amuck and shot a very important official.

A lot of windows broke in New York City the next day when a goodly portion of a county in Pennsylvania went up fast and came down slowly. No one within several hundred miles needed to be told that there was—or had been —a dump of A-bombs there. It was in sparsely populated country and not many people were killed, only a few thousand.

That was the afternoon, too, that the president of the stock exchange cut his throat and the crash started. Nobody paid too much attention to the riot at Lake Success the next day because of the unidentified submarine fleet that suddenly sank practically all the shipping in New Orleans harbor.

It was the evening of that day that Bill Wheeler was pacing up and down the front room of his apartment. Occasionally he stopped at the window to pet the Siamese named Beautiful and to look out across Central Park, bright under lights and cordoned off by armed sentries, where they were pouring concrete for the anti-aircraft gun emplacements.

He looked haggard.

He said, "Beautiful, we saw the start of it, right from this window. Maybe I'm crazy, but I still think that spaceship started it. God knows how. Maybe I should have fed you that mouse. Things couldn't have gone to pot so *suddenly* without help from somebody or something."

He shook his head slowly. "Let's dope it out, Beautiful. Let's say something came in on that ship besides a dead mouse. What could it have been? What could it have done and be doing?

"Let's say that the mouse was a laboratory animal, a guinea pig. It was sent in the ship and it survived the journey but died when it got here. Why? I've got a screwy hunch, Beautiful."

He sat down in a chair and leaned back, staring up at

the ceiling. He said, "Suppose the superior intelligence—
from Somewhere—that made that ship came in with it.
Suppose it wasn't the mouse—let's call it a mouse. Then,
since the mouse was the only physical thing in the spaceship, the being, the invader, wasn't physical. It was an
entity that could live apart from whatever body it had
back where it came from. But let's say it could live in *any*
body and it left its own in a safe place back home and rode
here in one that was expendable, that it could abandon on
arrival. That would explain the mouse and the fact that it
died at the time the ship landed.

"Then the *being,* at that instant, just jumped into the
body of someone here—probably one of the first people to
run toward the ship when it landed. It's living in somebody's body—in a hotel on Broadway or a flophouse on
the Bowery or anywhere—pretending to be a human being.
That make sense, Beautiful?"

He got up and started to pace again.

"And having the ability to control other minds, it sets
about to make the world—the Earth—safe for Martians or
Venusians or whatever they are. It sees—after a few days
of study—that the world is on the brink of destroying itself
and needs only a push. So it could give that push.

"It could get inside a nut and make him assassinate the
President, and get caught at it. It could make a Russian
shoot his Number 1. It could make a Spaniard shoot the
prime minister of England. It could start a bloody riot in
the U. N., and make an army man, there to guard it, explode an A-bomb dump. It could—hell, Beautiful, it could
push this world into a final war within a week. It practically
has done it."

He walked over to the window and stroked the cat's
sleek fur while he frowned down at the gun emplacements
going up under the bright floodlights.

"And he's done it and even if my guess is right I couldn't
stop him because I couldn't find him. And nobody would
believe me, now. He'll make the world safe for Martians.
When the war is over, a lot of little ships like that—or big
ones—can land here and take over what's left ten times as
easy as they could now."

He lighted a cigarette with hands that shook a little. He
said, "The more I think of it, the more—"

He sat down in the chair again. He said, "Beautiful, I've got to *try*. Screwy as that idea is, I've got to give it to the authorities, whether they believe it or not. That Major I met was an intelligent guy. So is General Keely. I—"

He started to walk to the phone and then sat down again. "I'll call both of them, but let's work it out just a little finer first. See if I can make any intelligent suggestions how they could go about finding the—the *being*—"

He groaned. "Beautiful, it's impossible. It wouldn't even have to be a human being. It could be an animal, anything. It could be you. He'd probably take over whatever nearby type of mind was nearest his own. If he was remotely feline, you'd have been the nearest cat."

He sat up and stared at her. He said, "I'm going crazy, Beautiful. I'm remembering how you jumped and twisted just after that spaceship blew up its mechanism and went inert. And, listen, Beautiful, you've been sleeping twice as much as usual lately. Has your mind been out—

"Say, *that* would be why I couldn't wake you up yesterday to feed you. Beautiful, cats always wake up easily. *Cats* do."

Looking dazed, Bill Wheeler got up out of the chair. He said, "Cat, *am* I crazy, or—"

The Siamese cat looked at him languidly through sleepy eyes. Distinctly it said, *"Forget it."*

And halfway between sitting and rising, Bill Wheeler looked even more dazed for a second. He shook his head as though to clear it.

He said, "What was I talking about, Beautiful? I'm getting punchy from not enough sleep."

He walked over to the window and stared out, gloomily, rubbing the cat's fur until it purred.

He said, "Hungry, Beautiful? Want some liver?"

The cat jumped down from the windowsill and rubbed itself against his leg affectionately.

It said, "Miaouw."

NATURALLY

HENRY BLODGETT looked at his wrist watch and saw that it was two o'clock in the morning. In despair, he slammed shut the textbook he'd been studying and let his head sink onto his arms on the table in front of him. He knew he'd never pass that examination tomorrow; the more he studied geometry the less he understood it. Mathematics in general had always been difficult for him and now he was finding that geometry was impossible for him to learn.

And if he flunked it, he was through with college; he'd flunked three other courses in his first two years and another failure this year would, under college rules, cause automatic expulsion.

He wanted that college degree badly too, since it was indispensable for the career he'd chosen and worked toward. Only a miracle could save him now.

He sat up suddenly as an idea struck him. Why not try magic? The occult had always interested him. He had books on it and he'd often read the simple instructions on how to conjure up a demon and make it obey his will. Up to now, he'd always figured that it was a bit risky and so had never actually tried it. But this was an emergency and might be worth the slight risk. Only through black magic could he suddenly become an expert in a subject that had always been difficult for him.

From the shelf he quickly took out his best book on black magic, found the right page and refreshed his memory on the few simple things he had to do.

Enthusiastically, he cleared the floor by pushing the furniture against the walls. He drew the pentagram figure on the carpet with chalk and stepped inside it. He then said the incantations.

The demon was considerably more horrible than he had anticipated. But he mustered his courage and started to explain his dilemma.

"I've always been poor at geometry," he began . . .

"You're telling *me*," said the demon gleefully.

Smiling flames, it came for him across the chalk lines of the useless hexagram Henry had drawn by mistake instead of the protecting pentagram.

VOODOO

Mʀ. Dᴇᴄᴋᴇʀ's wife had just returned from a trip to Haiti—a trip she had taken alone—to give them a cooling off period before they discussed a divorce.

It hadn't worked. Neither of them had cooled off in the slightest. In fact, they were finding now that they hated one another more than ever.

"Half," said Mrs. Decker firmly. "I'll not settle for anything less than half the money plus half the property."

"Ridiculous!" said Mr. Decker.

"Is it? I could have it all, you know. And quite easily, too. I studied voodoo while in Haiti."

"Rot!" said Mr. Decker.

"It isn't. And you should be glad that I am a good woman for I could kill you quite easily if I wished. I would then have *all* the money and *all* the real estate, and without any fear of consequences. A death accomplished by voodoo can not be distinguished from a death by heart failure."

"Rubbish!" said Mr. Decker.

"You think so? I have wax and a hatpin. Do you want to give me a tiny pinch of your hair or a fingernail clipping or two—that's all I need—and let me show you?"

"Nonsense!" said Mr. Decker.

"Then why are you afraid to have me try? Since *I* know it works, I'll make you a proposition. If it doesn't kill you, I'll give you a divorce and ask for nothing. If it does, I'll get it all automatically."

"Done!" said Mr. Decker. "Get your wax and hatpin." He glanced at his fingernails. "Pretty short. I'll give you a bit of hair."

When he came back with a few short strands of hair

in the lid of an aspirin tin, Mrs. Decker had already started softening the wax. She kneaded the hair into it, then shaped it into the rough effigy of a human being.

"You'll be sorry," she said, and thrust the hatpin into the chest of the wax figure.

Mr. Decker was surprised, but he was more pleased than sorry. He had not believed in voodoo, but being a cautious man he never took chances.

Besides, it had always irritated him that his wife so seldom cleaned her hairbrush.

"ARENA"

CARSON opened his eyes, and found himself looking upward into a flickering blue dimness.

It was hot, and he was lying on sand, and a sharp rock embedded in the sand was hurting his back. He rolled over to his side, off the rock, and then pushed himself up to a sitting position.

"I'm crazy," he thought. "Crazy—or dead—or something." The sand was blue, bright blue. And there wasn't any such thing as bright blue sand on Earth or any of the planets.

Blue sand.

Blue sand under a blue dome that wasn't the sky nor yet a room, but a circumscribed area—somehow he knew it was circumscribed and finite even though he couldn't see to the top of it.

He picked up some of the sand in his hand and let it run through his fingers. It trickled down onto his bare leg. *Bare?*

Naked. He was stark naked, and already his body was dripping perspiration from the enervating heat, coated blue with sand wherever sand had touched it.

But elsewhere his body was white.

He thought: Then this sand is really blue. If it seemed blue only because of the blue light, then I'd be blue also. But I'm white, so the sand *is* blue. *Blue sand.* There isn't any blue sand. There isn't any place like this place I'm in.

Sweat was running down in his eyes.

It was hot, hotter than hell. Only hell—the hell of the ancients—was supposed to be red and not blue.

But if this place wasn't hell, what was it? Only Mercury,

among the planets, had heat like this and this wasn't Mercury. And Mercury was some four billion miles from—

It came back to him then, where he'd been. In the little one-man scouter, outside the orbit of Pluto, scouting a scant million miles to one side of the Earth Armada drawn up in battle array there to intercept the Outsiders.

That sudden strident nerve-shattering ringing of the alarm bell when the rival scouter—the Outsider ship—had come within range of his detectors—

No one knew who the Outsiders were, what they looked like, from what far galaxy they came, other than that it was in the general direction of the Pleiades.

First, sporadic raids on Earth colonies and outposts. Isolated battles between Earth patrols and small groups of Outsider spaceships; battles sometimes won and sometimes lost, but never to date resulting in the capture of an alien vessel. Nor had any member of a raided colony ever survived to describe the Outsiders who had left the ships, if indeed they had left them.

Not a too-serious menace, at first, for the raids had not been too numerous or destructive. And individually, the ships had proved slightly inferior in armament to the best of Earth's fighters, although somewhat superor in speed and maneuverability. A sufficient edge in speed, in fact, to give the Outsiders their choice of running or fighting, unless surrounded.

Nevertheless, Earth had prepared for serious trouble, for a showdown, building the mightiest armada of all time. It had been waiting now, that armada, for a long time. But now the showdown was coming.

Scouts twenty billion miles out had detected the approach of a mighty fleet—a showdown fleet—of the Outsiders. Those scouts had never come back, but their radiotronic messages had. And now Earth's armada, all ten thousand ships and half-million fighting spacemen, was out there, outside Pluto's orbit, waiting to intercept and battle to the death.

And an even battle it was going to be, judging by the advance reports of the men of the far picket line who had given their lives to report—before they had died—on the size and strength of the alien fleet.

Anybody's battle, with the mastery of the solar system

hanging in the balance, on an even chance. A last and *only* chance, for Earth and all her colonies lay at the utter mercy of the Outsiders if they ran that gauntlet—

Oh yes. Bob Carson remembered now.

Not that it explained blue sand and flickering blueness. But that strident alarming of the bell and his leap for the control panel. His frenzied fumbling as he strapped himself into the seat. The dot in the visiplate that grew larger.

The dryness of his mouth. The awful knowledge that this was *it*. For him, at least, although the main fleets were still out of range of one another.

This, his first taste of battle. Within three seconds or less he'd be victorious, or a charred cinder. Dead.

Three seconds—that's how long a space-battle lasted. Time enough to count to three, slowly, and then you'd won or you were dead. One hit completely took care of a lightly armed and armored little one-man craft like a scouter.

Frantically—as, unconsciously, his dry lips shaped the word "One"—he worked at the controls to keep that growing dot centered on the crossed spiderwebs of the visiplate. His hands doing that, while his right foot hovered over the pedal that would fire the bolt. The single bolt of concentrated hell that had to hit—or else. There wouldn't be time for any second shot.

"Two." He didn't know he'd said that, either. The dot in the visiplate wasn't a dot now. Only a few thousand miles away, it showed up in the magnification of the plate as though it were only a few hundred yards off. It was a sleek, fast little scouter, about the size of his.

And an alien ship, all right.

"Thr—" His foot touched the bolt-release pedal—

And then the Outsider had swerved suddenly and was off the crosshairs. Carson punched keys frantically, to follow.

For a tenth of a second, it was out of the visiplate entirely, and then as the nose of his scouter swung after it, he saw it again, diving straight toward the ground.

The ground?

It was an optical illusion of some sort. It *had* to be, that planet—or whatever it was—that now covered the visiplate. Whatever it was, it couldn't be there. Couldn't possibly. There *wasn't* any planet nearer than Neptune three billion miles away—with Pluto around on the opposite side of the distant pinpoint sun.

His *detectors! They* hadn't shown any object of planetary dimensions, even of asteroid dimensions. They still didn't.

So it couldn't be there, that whatever-it-was he was driving into, only a few hundred miles below him.

And in his sudden anxiety to keep from crashing, he forgot even the Outsider ship. He fired the front braking rockets, and even as the sudden change of speed slammed him forward against the seat straps, he fired full right for an emergency turn. Pushed them down and *held* them down, knowing that he needed everything the ship had to keep from crashing and that a turn that sudden would black him out for a moment.

It did black him out.

And that was all. Now he was sitting in hot blue sand, stark naked but otherwise unhurt. No sign of his spaceship and—for that matter—no sign of *space*. That curve overhead wasn't a sky, whatever else it was.

He scrambled to his feet.

Gravity seemed a little more than Earth-normal. Not much more.

Flat sand stretching away, a few scrawny bushes in clumps here and there. The bushes were blue, too, but in varying shades, some lighter than the blue of the sand, some darker.

Out from under the nearest bush ran a little thing that was like a lizard, except that it had more than four legs. It was blue, too. Bright blue. It saw him and ran back again under the bush.

He looked up again, trying to decide what was overhead. It wasn't exactly a roof, but it was dome-shaped. It flickered and was hard to look at. But definitely, it curved down to the ground, to the blue sand, all around him.

He wasn't far from being under the center of the dome. At a guess, it was a hundred yards to the nearest wall, if it was a wall. It was as though a blue hemisphere of *something,* about two hundred and fifty yards in circumference, was inverted over the flat expanse of the sand.

And everything blue, except one object. Over near a far curving wall there was a red object. Roughly spherical, it seemed to be about a yard in diameter. Too far for him to see clearly through the flickering blueness. But, unaccountably, he shuddered.

He wiped sweat from his forehead, or tried to, with the back of his hand.

Was this a dream, a nightmare? This heat, this sand, that vague feeling of horror he felt when he looked toward that red thing?

A dream? No, one didn't go to sleep and dream in the midst of a battle in space.

Death? No, never. If there were immortality, it wouldn't be a senseless thing like this, a thing of blue heat and blue sand and a red horror.

Then he heard the voice—

Inside his head he heard it, not with his ears. It came from nowhere or everywhere.

"Through spaces and dimensions wandering," rang the words in his mind, *"and in this space and this time I find two peoples about to wage a war that would exterminate one and so weaken the other that it would retrogress and never fulfill its destiny, but decay and return to mindless dust whence it came. And I say this must not happen."*

"Who . . . what are you?" Carson didn't say it aloud, but the question formed itself in his brain.

"You would not understand completely. I am—" There was a pause as though the voice sought—in Carson's brain—for a word that wasn't there, a word he didn't know. *"I am the end of evolution of a race so old the time can not be expressed in words that have meaning to your mind. A race fused into a single entity, eternal—*

"An entity such as your primitive race might become"—again the groping for a word—*"time from now. So might the race you call, in your mind, the Outsiders. So I intervene in the battle to come, the battle between fleets so evenly matched that destruction of both races will result. One must survive. One must progress and evolve."*

"One?" thought Carson. "Mine, or—?"

"It is in my power to stop the war, to send the Outsiders back to their galaxy. But they would return, or your race would sooner or later follow them there. Only by remain-

ing in this space and time to intervene constantly could I prevent them from destroying one another, and I cannot remain.

"So I shall intervene now. I shall destroy one fleet completely without loss to the other. One civilization shall thus survive."

Nightmare. This had to be nightmare, Carson thought. But he knew it wasn't.

It was too mad, too impossible, to be anything but real.

He didn't dare ask *the* question—*which?* But his thoughts asked it for him.

"*The stronger shall survive,*" said the voice. "*That I can not—and would not—change. I merely intervene to make it a complete victory, not*"—groping again—"*not Pyrrhic victory to a broken race.*

"*From the outskirts of the not-yet battle I plucked two individuals, you and an Outsider. I see from your mind that in your early history of nationalisms battles between champions, to decide issues between races, were not unknown.*

"*You and your opponent are here pitted against one another, naked and unarmed, under conditions equally unfamiliar to you both, equally unpleasant to you both. There is no time limit, for here there is no time. The survivor is the champion of his race. That race survives.*"

"But—" Carson's protest was too inarticulate for expression, but the voice answered it.

"*It is fair. The conditions are such that the accident of physical strength will not completely decide the issue. There is a barrier. You will understand. Brain-power and courage will be more important than strength. Most especially courage, which is the will to survive.*"

"But while this goes on, the fleets will—"

"*No, you are in another space, another time. For as long as you are here, time stands still in the universe you know. I see you wonder whether this place is real. It is, and it is not. As I—to your limited understanding—am and am not real. My existence is mental and not physical. You saw me as a planet; it could have been as a dust-mote or a sun.*

"*But to you this place is now real. What you suffer here*

*will be real. And if you die here, your death will be real.
If you die, your failure will be the end of your race. That
is enough for you to know."*

And then the voice was gone.

Again he was alone, but not alone. For as Carson
looked up, he saw that the red thing, the red sphere of
horror which he now knew was the Outsider, was rolling
toward him.

Rolling.

It seemed to have no legs or arms that he could see,
no features. It rolled across the blue sand with the fluid
quickness of a drop of mercury. And before it, in some
manner he could not understand, came a paralyzing wave
of nauseating, retching, horrid hatred.

Carson looked about him frantically. A stone, lying
in the sand a few feet away, was the nearest thing to a
weapon. It wasn't large, but it had sharp edges, like a slab
of flint. It looked a bit like blue flint.

He picked it up, and crouched to receive the attack.
It was coming fast, faster than he could run.

No time to think out how he was going to fight it, and
how anyway could he plan to battle a creature whose
strength, whose characteristics, whose method of fighting
he did not know? Rolling so fast, it looked more than ever
like a perfect sphere.

Ten yards away. Five. And then it stopped.

Rather, it *was stopped*. Abruptly the near side of it
flattened as though it had run up against an invisible wall.
It bounced, actually bounced back.

Then it rolled forward again, but more slowly, more cautiously. It stopped again, at the same place. It tried again,
a few yards to one side.

There was a barrier there of some sort. It clicked, then,
in Carson's mind. That thought projected into his mind
by the Entity who had brought them here: "—accident of
physical strength will not completely decide the issue.
There is a barrier."

A force-field, of course. Not the Netzian Field, known
to Earth science, for that glowed and emitted a crackling
sound. This one was invisible, silent.

It was a wall that ran from side to side of the inverted

hemisphere; Carson didn't have to verify that himself. The Roller was doing that; rolling sideways along the barrier, seeking a break in it that wasn't there.

Carson took half a dozen steps forward, his left hand groping out before him, and then his hand touched the barrier. It felt smooth, yielding, like a sheet of rubber rather than like glass. Warm to his touch, but no warmer than the sand underfoot. And it was completely invisible, even at close range.

He dropped the stone and put both hands against it, pushing. It seemed to yield, just a trifle. But no farther than that trifle, even when he pushed with all his weight. It felt like a sheet of rubber backed up by steel. Limited resiliency, and then firm strength.

He stood on tiptoe and reached as high as he could and the barrier was still there.

He saw the Roller coming back, having reached one side of the arena. That feeling of nausea hit Carson again, and he stepped back from the barrier as it went by. It didn't stop.

But did the barrier stop at ground level? Carson knelt down and burrowed in the sand. It was soft, light, easy to dig in. At two feet down the barrier was still there.

The Roller was coming back again. Obviously, it couldn't find a way through at either side.

There must be a way through, Carson thought. *Some way we can get at each other, else this duel is meaningless.*

But no hurry now, in finding that out. There was something to try first. The Roller was back now, and it stopped just across the barrier, only six feet away. It seemed to be studying him, although for the life of him, Carson couldn't find external evidence of sense organs on the thing. Nothing that looked like eyes or ears, or even a mouth. There was though, he saw now, a series of grooves—perhaps a dozen of them altogether, and he saw two tentacles suddenly push out from two of the grooves and dip into the sand as though testing its consistency. Tentacles about an inch in diameter and perhaps a foot and a half long.

But the tentacles were retractable into the grooves and were kept there except when not in use. They were retracted when the thing rolled and seemed to have nothing to do with its method of locomotion. That, as far as Carson could judge, seemed to be accomplished by some shifting—just *how* he couldn't even imagine—of its center of gravity.

He shuddered as he looked at the thing. It was alien, utterly alien, horribly different from anything on Earth or any of the life forms found on the other solar planets. Instinctively, somehow, he knew its mind was as alien as its body.

But he had to try. If it had no telepathic powers at all, the attempt was foredoomed to failure, yet he thought it had such powers. There had, at any rate, been a projection of something that was not physical at the time a few minutes ago when it had first started for him. An almost tangible wave of hatred.

If it could project that, perhaps it could read his mind as well, sufficiently for his purpose.

Deliberately, Carson picked up the rock that had been his only weapon, then tossed it down again in a gesture of relinquishment and raised his empty hands, palms up, before him.

He spoke aloud, knowing that although the words would be meaningless to the creature before him, speaking them would focus his own thoughts more completely upon the message.

"Can we not have peace between us?" he said, his voice sounding strange in the utter stillness. "The Entity who brought us here has told us what must happen if our races fight—extinction of one and weakening and retrogression of the other. The battle between them, said the Entity, depends upon what we do here. Why can not we agree to an eternal peace—your race to its galaxy, we to ours?"

Carson blanked out his mind to receive a reply.

It came, and it staggered him back, physically. He actually recoiled several steps in sheer horror at the depth and intensity of the hatred and lust-to-kill of the red images that had been projected at him. Not as articulate words—as had come to him the thoughts of the Entity—but as wave upon wave of fierce emotion.

For a moment that seemed an eternity he had to struggle against the mental impact of that hatred, fight to clear his mind of it and drive out the alien thoughts to which he had given admittance by blanking his own thoughts. He wanted to retch.

Slowly his mind cleared as, slowly, the mind of a man wakening from nightmare clears away the fear-fabric of which the dream was woven. He was breathing hard and he felt weaker, but he could think.

He stood studying the Roller. It had been motionless during the mental duel it had so nearly won. Now it rolled a few feet to one side, to the nearest of the blue bushes. Three tentacles whipped out of their grooves and began to investigate the bush.

"O. K.," Carson said, "so it's war then." He managed a wry grin. "If I got your answer straight, peace doesn't appeal to you." And, because he was, after all, a quite young man and couldn't resist the impulse to be dramatic, he added. "To the death!"

But his voice, in that utter silence, sounded very silly, even to himself. It came to him, then, that this *was* to the death. Not only his own death or that of the red spherical thing which he now thought of as the Roller, but death to the entire race of one or the other of them. The end of the human race, if he failed.

It made him suddenly very humble and very afraid to think that. More than to think it, to *know* it. Somehow, with a knowledge that was above even faith, he knew that the Entity who had arranged this duel had told the truth about its intentions and it powers. It wasn't kidding.

The future of humanity depended upon *him*. It was an awful thing to realize, and he wrenched his mind away from it. He had to concentrate on the situation at hand.

There had to be some way of getting through the barrier, or of killing through the barrier.

Mentally? He hoped that wasn't all, for the Roller obviously had stronger telepathic powers than the primitive, undeveloped ones of the human race. Or did it?

He had been able to drive the thoughts of the Roller out of his own mind; could it drive out his? If its ability to project were stronger, might not its receptivity mechanism be more vulnerable?

He stared at it and endeavored to concentrate and focus all his thoughts upon it.

"Die," he thought. *"You are going to die. You are dying. You are—"*

He tried variations on it, and mental pictures. Sweat stood out on his forehead and he found himself trembling with the intensity of the effort. But the Roller went ahead with its investigation of the bush, as utterly unaffected as though Carson had been reciting the multiplication table.

So *that* was no good.

He felt a bit weak and dizzy from the heat and his strenuous effort at concentration. He sat down on the blue sand to rest and gave his full attention to watching and studying the Roller. By close study, perhaps, he could judge its strength and detect its weaknesses, learn things that would be valuable to know when and if they should come to grips.

It was breaking off twigs. Carson watched carefully, trying to judge just how hard it worked to do that. Later, he thought, he could find a similar bush on his own side, break off twigs of equal thickness himself, and gain a comparison of physical strength between his own arms and hands and those tentacles.

The twigs broke off hard; the Roller was having to struggle with each one, he saw. Each tentacle, he saw, bifurcated at the tip into two fingers, each tipped by a nail or claw. The claws didn't seem to be particularly long or dangerous. No more so than his own fingernails, if they were let to grow a bit.

No, on the whole, it didn't look too tough to handle physically. Unless, of course, that bush was made of pretty tough stuff. Carson looked around him and, yes, right within reach was another bush of indentically the same type.

He reached over and snapped off a twig. It was brittle, easy to break. Of course, the Roller might have been faking deliberately but he didn't think so.

On the other hand, where was it vulnerable? Just how would he go about killing it, if he got the chance? He went back to studying it. The outer hide looked pretty tough. He'd need a sharp weapon of some sort. He picked up the piece of rock again. It was about twelve inches long, narrow, and fairly sharp on one end. If it chipped like flint, he could make a serviceable knife out of it.

The Roller was continuing its investigations of the bushes. It rolled again, to the nearest one of another type. A little blue lizard, many-legged like the one Carson had seen on his side of the barrier, darted out from under the bush.

A tentacle of the Roller lashed out and caught it, picked it up. Another tentacle whipped over and began to pull legs off the lizard, as coldly and calmly as it had pulled twigs off the bush. The creature struggled frantically and emitted a shrill squealing sound that was the first sound Carson had heard here other than the sound of his own voice.

Carson shuddered and wanted to turn his eyes away. But he made himself continue to watch; anything he could learn about his opponent might prove valuable. Even this knowledge of its unnecessary cruelty. Particularly, he thought with a sudden vicious surge of emotion, this knowledge of its unnecessary cruelty. It would make it a pleasure to kill the thing, if and when the chance came.

He steeled himself to watch the dismembering of the lizard, for that very reason.

But he felt glad when, with half its legs gone, the lizard quit squealing and struggling and lay limp and dead in the Roller's grasp.

It didn't continue with the rest of the legs. Contemptuously it tossed the dead lizard away from it, in Carson's direction. It arced through the air between them and landed at his feet.

It had come through the barrier! The barrier wasn't there any more!

Carson was on his feet in a flash, the knife gripped tightly in his hand, and leaped forward. He'd settle this thing here and now! With the barrier gone—

But it wasn't gone. He found that out the hard way, running head on into it and nearly knocking himself silly. He bounced back, and fell.

And as he sat up, shaking his head to clear it, he saw something coming through the air toward him, and to duck it, he threw himself flat again on the sand, and to one side. He got his body out of the way, but there was a sudden sharp pain in the calf of his left leg.

He rolled backward, ignoring the pain, and scrambled

to his feet. It was a rock, he saw now, that had struck him. And the Roller was picking up another one now, swinging it back gripped between two tentacles, getting ready to throw again.

It sailed through the air toward him, but he was easily able to step out of its way. The Roller, apparently, could throw straight, but not hard nor far. The first rock had struck him only because he had been sitting down and had not seen it coming until it was almost upon him.

Even as he stepped aside from that weak second throw, Carson drew back his right arm and let fly with the rock that was still in his hand. If missiles, he thought with sudden elation, can cross the barrier, then two can play at the game of throwing them. And the good right arm of an Earthman—

He couldn't miss a three-foot sphere at only four-yard range, and he didn't miss. The rock whizzed straight, and with a speed several times that of the missiles the Roller had thrown. It hit dead center, but it hit flat, unfortunately, instead of point first.

But it hit with a resounding thump, and obviously it hurt. The Roller had been reaching for another rock, but it changed its mind and got out of there instead. By the time Carson could pick up and throw another rock, the Roller was forty yards back from the barrier and going strong.

His second throw missed by feet, and his third throw was short. The Roller was back out of range—at least out of range of a missile heavy enough to be damaging.

Carson grinned. That round had been his. Except—

He quit grinning as he bent over to examine the calf of his leg. A jagged edge of the stone had made a pretty deep cut, several inches long. It was bleeding pretty freely, but he didn't think it had gone deep enough to hit an artery. If it stopped bleeding of its own accord, well and good. If not, he was in for trouble.

Finding out one thing, though, took precedence over that cut. The nature of the barrier.

He went forward to it again, this time groping with his hands before him. He found it; then holding one hand against it, he tossed a handful of sand at it with the other hand. The sand went right through. His hand didn't.

Organic matter versus inorganic? No, because the dead lizard had gone through it, and a lizard, alive or dead, was certainly organic. Plant life? He broke off a twig and poked it at the barrier. The twig went through, with no resistance, but when his fingers gripping the twig came to the barrier, they were stopped.

He couldn't get through it, nor could the Roller. But rocks and sand and a dead lizard—

How about a live lizard? He went hunting, under bushes, until he found one, and caught it. He tossed it gently against the barrier and it bounced back and scurried away across the blue sand.

That gave him the answer, in so far as he could determine it now. The screen was a barrier to living things. Dead or inorganic matter could cross it.

That off his mind, Carson looked at his injured leg again. The bleeding was lessening, which meant he wouldn't need to worry about making a tourniquet. But he should find some water, if any was available, to clean the wound.

Water—the thought of it made him realize that he was getting awfully thirsty. He'd *have* to find water, in case this contest turned out to be a protracted one.

Limping slightly now, he started off to make a full circuit of his half of the arena. Guiding himself with one hand along the barrier, he walked to his right until he came to the curving sidewall. It was visible, a dull blue-gray at close range, and the surface of it felt just like the central barrier.

He experimented by tossing a handful of sand at it, and the sand reached the wall and disappeared as it went through. The hemispherical shell was a force-field, too. But an opaque one, instead of transparent like the barrier.

He followed it around until he came back to the barrier, and walked back along the barrier to the point from which he'd started.

No sign of water.

Worried now, he started a series of zigzags back and forth between the barrier and the wall, covering the intervening space thoroughly.

No water. Blue sand, blue bushes, and intolerable heat. Nothing else.

It must be his imagination, he told himself angrily, that

he was suffering *that* much from thirst. How long had he been here? Of course, no time at all, according to his own space-time frame. The Entity had told him time stood still out there, while he was here. But his body processes went on here, just the same. And according to his body's reckoning, how long had he been here? Three or four hours, perhaps. Certainly not long enough to be suffering seriously from thirst.

But he was suffering from it; his throat dry and parched. Probably the intense heat was the cause. It was *hot!* A hundred and thirty Fahrenheit, at a guess. A dry, still heat without the slightest movement of air.

He was limping rather badly, and utterly fagged out when he'd finished the futile exploration of his domain.

He stared across at the motionless Roller and hoped it was as miserable as he was. And quite possibly it wasn't enjoying this, either. The Entity had said the conditions here were equally unfamiliar and equally uncomfortable for both of them. Maybe the Roller came from a planet where two-hundred degree heat was the norm. Maybe it was freezing while he was roasting.

Maybe the air was as much too thick for it as it was too thin for him. For the exertion of his explorations had left him panting. The atmosphere here, he realized now, was not much thicker than that on Mars.

No water.

That meant a deadline, for him at any rate. Unless he could find a way to cross that barrier or to kill his enemy from this side of it, thirst would kill him, eventually.

It gave him a feeling of desperate urgency. He *must* hurry.

But he made himself sit down a moment to rest, to think.

What was there to do? Nothing, and yet so many things. The several varieties of bushes, for example. They didn't look promising, but he'd have to examine them for possibilities. And his leg—he'd have to do something about that, even without water to clean it. Gather ammunition in the form of rocks. Find a rock that would make a good knife.

His leg hurt rather badly now, and he decided that came first. One type of bush had leaves—or things rather similar to leaves. He pulled off a handful of them and decided, after examination, to take a chance on them. He used them to clean off the sand and dirt and caked blood, then made a pad of fresh leaves and tied it over the wound with tendrils from the same bush.

The tendrils proved unexpectedly tough and strong. They were slender, and soft and pliable, yet he couldn't break them at all. He had to saw them off the bush with the sharp edge of a piece of the blue flint. Some of the thicker ones were over a foot long, and he filed away in his memory, for future reference, the fact that a bunch of the thick ones, tied together, would make a pretty serviceable rope. Maybe he'd be able to think of a use for rope.

Next, he made himself a knife. The blue flint *did* chip. From a foot-long splinter of it, he fashioned himself a crude but lethal weapon. And of tendrils from the bush, he made himself a rope-belt through which he could thrust the flint knife, to keep it with him all the time and yet have his hands free.

He went back to studying the bushes. There were three other types. One was leafless, dry, brittle, rather like a dried tumbleweed. Another was of soft, crumbly wood, almost like punk. It looked and felt as though it would make excellent tinder for a fire. The third type was the most nearly woodlike. It had fragile leaves that wilted at a touch, but the stalks, although short, were straight and strong.

It was horribly, unbearably hot.

He limped up to the barrier, felt to make sure that it was still there. It was.

He stood watching the Roller for a while. It was keeping a safe distance back from the barrier, out of effective stone-throwing range. It was moving around back there, doing something. He couldn't tell what it was doing.

Once it stopped moving, came a little closer, and seemed to concentrate its attention on him. Again Carson had to fight off a wave of nausea. He threw a stone at it and the Roller retreated and went back to whatever it had been doing before.

At least he could make it keep its distance.

And, he thought bitterly, a devil of a lot of good *that*

did him. Just the same, he spent the next hour or two gathering stones of suitable size for throwing, and making several neat piles of them, near his side of the barrier.

His throat burned now. It was difficult for him to think about anything except water.

But he *had* to think about other things. About getting through that barrier, under or over it, getting *at* that red sphere and killing it before this place of heat and thirst killed him first.

The barrier went to the wall upon either side, but how high and how far under the sand?

For just a moment, Carson's mind was too fuzzy to think out how he could find out either of those things. Idly, sitting there in the hot sand—and he didn't remember sitting down—he watched a blue lizard crawl from the shelter of one bush to the shelter of another.

From under the second bush, it looked out at him.

Carson grinned at it. Maybe he was getting a bit punch-drunk, because he remembered suddenly the old story of the desert-colonists on Mars, taken from an older desert story of Earth— "Pretty soon you get so lonesome you find yourself talking to the lizards, and then not so long after that you find the lizards talking back to you—"

He should have been concentrating, of course, on how to kill the Roller, but instead he grinned at the lizard and said, "Hello, there."

The lizard took a few steps toward him. "Hello," it said.

Carson was stunned for a moment, and then he put back his head and roared with laughter. It didn't hurt his throat to do so, either; he hadn't been *that* thirsty.

Why not? Why should the Entity who thought up this nightmare of a place not have a sense of humor, along with the other powers he has? Talking lizards, equipped to talk back in my own language, if I talk to them— It's a nice touch.

He grinned at the lizard and said, "Come on over." But the lizard turned and ran away, scurrying from bush to bush until it was out of sight.

He was thirsty again.

And he had to *do* something. He couldn't win this contest by sitting here sweating and feeling miserable. He had to *do* something. But what?

Get through the barrier. But he couldn't get through it, or over it. But was he certain he couldn't get under it? And come to think of it, didn't one sometimes find water by digging? Two birds with one stone—

Painfully now, Carson limped up to the barrier and started digging, scooping up sand a double handful at a time. It was slow, hard work because the sand ran in at the edges and the deeper he got the bigger in diameter the hole had to be. How many hours it took him, he didn't know, but he hit bedrock four feet down. Dry bedrock; no sign of water.

And the force-field of the barrier went down clear to the bedrock. No dice. No water. Nothing.

He crawled out of the hole and lay there panting, and then raised his head to look across and see what the Roller was doing. It must be doing something back there.

It was. It was making something out of wood from the bushes, tied together with tendrils. A queerly shaped framework about four feet high and roughly square. To see it better, Carson climbed up onto the mound of sand he had excavated from the hole, and stood there staring.

There were two long levers sticking out of the back of it, one with a cup-shaped affair on the end of it. Seemed to be some sort of a catapult, Carson thought.

Sure enough, the Roller was lifting a sizable rock into the cup-shaped outfit. One of his tentacles moved the other lever up and down for a while, and then he turned the machine slightly as though aiming it and the lever with the stone flew up and forward.

The stone arced several yards over Carson's head, so far away that he didn't have to duck, but he judged the distance it had traveled, and whistled softly. He couldn't throw a rock that weight more than half that distance. And even retreating to the rear of his domain wouldn't put him out of range of that machine, if the Roller shoved it forward almost to the barrier.

Another rock whizzed over. Not quite so far away this time.

That thing could be dangerous, he decided. Maybe he'd better do something about it.

Moving from side to side along the barrier, so the catapult couldn't bracket him, he whaled a dozen rocks at it.

But that wasn't going to be any good, he saw. They had to be light rocks, or he couldn't throw them that far. If they hit the framework, they bounced off harmlessly. And the Roller had no difficulty, at that distance, in moving aside from those that came near it.

Besides, his arm was tiring badly. He ached all over from sheer weariness. If he could only rest a while without having to duck rocks from that catapult at regular intervals of maybe thirty seconds each—

He stumbled back to the rear of the arena. Then he saw even that wasn't any good. The rocks reached back there, too, only there were longer intervals between them, as though it took longer to wind up the mechanism, whatever it was, of the catapult.

Wearily he dragged himself back to the barrier again. Several times he fell and could barely rise to his feet to go on. He was, he knew, near the limit of his endurance. Yet he didn't dare stop moving now, until and unless he could put that catapult out of action. If he fell asleep, he'd never wake up.

One of the stones from it gave him the first glimmer of an idea. It struck upon one of the piles of stones he'd gathered together near the barrier to use as ammunition, and it struck sparks.

Sparks. Fire. Primitive man had made fire by striking sparks, and with some of those dry crumbly bushes as tinder—

Luckily, a bush of that type was near him. He broke it off, took it over to the pile of stones, then patiently hit one stone against another until a spark touched the punk-like wood of the bush. It went up in flames so fast that it singed his eyebrows and was burned to an ash within seconds.

But he had the idea now, and within minutes he had a little fire going in the lee of the mound of sand he'd made digging the hole an hour or two ago. Tinder bushes had started it, and other bushes which burned, but more slowly, kept it a steady flame.

The tough wirelike tendrils didn't burn readily; that made the fire-bombs easy to make and throw. A bundle of faggots tied about a small stone to give it weight and a loop of the tendril to swing it by.

He made half a dozen of them before he lighted and threw the first. It went wide, and the Roller started a quick retreat, pulling the catapult after him. But Carson had the others ready and threw them in rapid succession. The fourth wedged in the catapult's frame work, and did the trick. The Roller tried desperately to put out the spreading blaze by throwing sand, but its clawed tentacles would take only a spoonful at a time and his efforts were ineffectual. The catapult burned.

The Roller moved safely away from the fire and seemed to concentrate its attention on Carson and again he felt that wave of hatred and nausea. But more weakly; either the Roller itself was weakening or Carson had learned how to protect himself against the mental attack.

He thumbed his nose at it and then sent it scuttling back to safety by throwing a stone. The Roller went clear to the back of its half of the arena and started pulling up bushes again. Probably it was going to make another catapult.

Carson verified—for the hundredth time—that the barrier was still operating, and then found himself sitting in the sand beside it because he was suddenly too weak to stand up.

His leg throbbed steadily now and the pangs of thirst were severe. But those things paled beside the utter physical exhaustion that gripped his entire body.

And the heat.

Hell must be like this, he thought. The hell that the ancients had believed in. He fought to stay awake, and yet staying awake seemed futile, for there was nothing he could do. Nothing, while the barrier remained impregnable and the Roller stayed back out of range.

But there must be *something*. He tried to remember things he had read in books of archaeology about the methods of fighting used back in the days before metal and plastic. The stone missile, that had come first, he thought. Well, that he already had.

The only improvement on it would be a catapult, such as the Roller had made. But he'd never be able to make one, with the tiny bits of wood available from the bushes—no single piece longer than a foot or so. Certainly he could figure out a mechanism for one, but he didn't have the endurance left for a task that would take days.

Days? But the Roller had made one. Had they been here days already? Then he remembered that the Roller had many tentacles to work with and undoubtedly could do such work faster than he.

And besides, a catapult wouldn't decide the issue. He had to do better than that.

Bow and arrow? No; he'd tried archery once and knew his own ineptness with a bow. Even with a modern sportsman's durasteel weapon, made for accuracy. With such a crude, pieced-together outfit as he could make here, he doubted if he could shoot as far as he could throw a rock, and knew he couldn't shoot as straight.

Spear? Well, he *could* make that. It would be useless as a throwing weapon at any distance, but would be a handy thing at close range, if he ever got to close range.

And making one would give him something to do. Help keep his mind from wandering, as it was beginning to do. Sometimes now, he had to concentrate a while before he could remember why he was here, why he had to kill the Roller.

Luckily he was still beside one of the piles of stones. He sorted through it until he found one shaped roughly like a spearhead. With a smaller stone he began to chip it into shape, fashioning sharp shoulders on the sides so that if it penetrated it would not pull out again.

Like a harpoon? There was something in that idea, he thought. A harpoon was better than a spear, maybe, for this crazy contest. If he could once get it into the Roller, and had a rope on it, he could pull the Roller up against the barrier and the stone blade of his knife would reach through that barrier, even if his hands wouldn't.

The shaft was harder to make than the head. But by splitting and joining the main stems of four of the bushes, and wrapping the joints with the tough but thin tendrils, he got a strong shaft about four feet long, and tied the stone head in a notch cut in the end.

It was crude, but strong.

And the rope. With the thin tough tendrils he made himself twenty feet of line. It was light and didn't look strong, but he knew it would hold his weight and to spare. He tied one end of it to the shaft of the harpoon and the other end about his right wrist. At least, if he threw his harpoon across the barrier, he'd be able to pull it back if he missed.

Then when he had tied the last knot and there was nothing more he could do, the heat and the weariness and the pain in his leg and the dreadful thirst were suddenly a thousand times worse than they had been before.

He tried to stand up, to see what the Roller was doing now, and found he couldn't get to his feet. On the third try, he got as far as his knees and then fell flat again.

"I've got to sleep," he thought. "If a showdown came now, I'd be helpless. He could come up here and kill me, if he knew. I've got to regain some strength."

Slowly, painfully, he crawled back away from the barrier. Ten yards, twenty—

The jar of something thudding against the sand near him waked him from a confused and horrible dream to a more confused and more horrible reality, and he opened his eyes again to blue radiance over blue sand.

How long had he slept? A minute? A day?

Another stone thudded nearer and threw sand on him. He got his arms under him and sat up. He turned around and saw the Roller twenty yards away, at the barrier.

It rolled away hastily as he sat up, not stopping until it was as far away as it could get.

He'd fallen asleep too soon, he realized, while he was still in range of the Roller's throwing ability. Seeing him lying motionless, it had dared come up to the barrier to throw at him. Luckily, it didn't realize how weak he was, or it could have stayed there and kept on throwing stones.

Had he slept long? He didn't think so, because he felt just as he had before. Not rested at all, no thirstier, no different. Probably he'd been there only a few minutes.

He started crawling again, this time forcing himself to keep going until he was as far as he could go, until the colorless, opaque wall of the arena's outer shell was only a yard away.

Then things slipped away again—

When he awoke, nothing about him was changed, but this time he knew that he had slept a long time.

The first thing he became aware of was the inside of his mouth; it was dry, caked. His tongue was swollen.

Something was wrong, he knew, as he returned slowly to full awareness. He felt less tired, the stage of utter exhaustion had passed. The sleep had taken care of that.

But there was pain, agonizing pain. It wasn't until he tried to move that he knew that it came from his leg.

He raised his head and looked down at it. It was swollen terribly below the knee and the swelling showed even halfway up his thigh. The plant tendrils he had used to tie on the protective pad of leaves now cut deeply into the swollen flesh.

To get his knife under that imbedded lashing would have been impossible. Fortunately, the final knot was over the shin bone, in front, where the vine cut in less deeply than elsewhere. He was able, after an agonizing effort, to untie the knot.

A look under the pad of leaves told him the worst. Infection and blood poisoning, both pretty bad and getting worse.

And without drugs, without cloth, without even *water*, there wasn't a thing he could do about it.

Not a thing, except *die,* when the poison had spread through his system.

He knew it was hopeless, then, and that he'd lost.

And with him, humanity. When he died here, out there in the universe he knew, all his friends, everybody, would die too. And Earth and the colonized planets would be the home of the red, rolling, alien Outsiders. Creatures out of nightmare, things without a human attribute, who picked lizards apart for the fun of it.

It was the thought of that which gave him courage to start crawling, almost blindly in pain, toward the barrier again. Not crawling on hands and knees this time, but pulling himself along only by his arms and hands.

A chance in a million, that maybe he'd have strength left, when he got there, to throw his harpoon-spear just *once,* and with deadly effect, if—on another chance in a million—the Roller would come up to the barrier. Or if the barrier was gone, now.

It took him years, it seemed, to get there.

The barrier wasn't gone. It was as impassable as when he'd first felt it.

And the Roller wasn't at the barrier. By raising up on his elbows, he could see it at the back of its part of the arena, working on a wooden framework that was a half-completed duplicate of the catapult he'd destroyed.

It was moving slowly now. Undoubtedly it had weakened, too.

But Carson doubted that it would ever need that second catapult. He'd be dead, he thought, before it was finished.

If he could attract it to the barrier, now, while he was still alive— He waved an arm and tried to shout, but his parched throat would make no sound.

Or if he could get through the barrier—

His mind must have slipped for a moment, for he found himself beating his fists against the barrier in futile rage, made himself stop.

He closed his eyes, tried to make himself calm.

"Hello," said the voice.

It was a small, thin voice. It sounded like—

He opened his eyes and turned his head. It *was* a lizard.

"Go away," Carson wanted to say. "Go away; you're not really there, or you're there but not really talking. I'm imagining things again."

But he couldn't talk; his throat and tongue were past all speech with the dryness. He closed his eyes again.

"Hurt," said the voice. "Kill. Hurt—kill. Come."

He opened his eyes again. The blue ten-legged lizard was still there. It ran a little way along the barrier, came back, started off again, and came back.

"Hurt," it said. "Kill. Come."

Again it started off, and came back. Obviously it wanted Carson to follow it along the barrier.

He closed his eyes again. The voice kept on. The same three meaningless words. Each time he opened his eyes, it ran off and came back.

"Hurt. Kill. Come."

Carson groaned. There would be no peace unless he followed the blasted thing. Like it wanted him to.

He followed it, crawling. Another sound, a high-pitched squealing, came to his ears and grew louder.

There was something lying in the sand, writhing, squealing. Something small, blue, that looked like a lizard and yet didn't—

Then he saw what it was—the lizard whose legs the Roller had pulled off, so long ago. But it wasn't dead; it had come back to life and was wriggling and screaming in agony.

"Hurt," said the other lizard. "Hurt. Kill. Kill."

Carson understood. He took the flint knife from his belt and killed the tortured creature. The live lizard scurried off quickly.

Carson turned back to the barrier. He leaned his hands and head against it and watched the Roller, far back, working on the new catapult.

"I could get that far," he thought, "If I could get through. If I could get through, I might win yet. It looks weak, too. I might—"

And then there was another reaction of black hopelessness, when pain sapped his will and he wished that he were dead. He envied the lizard he'd just killed. It didn't have to live on and suffer. And he did. It would be hours, it might be days, before the blood poisoning killed him.

If only he could use that knife on himself—

But he knew he wouldn't. As long as he was alive, there was the millionth chance—.

He was straining, pushing on the barrier with the flat of his hands, and he noticed his arms, how thin and scrawny they were now. He must really have been here a long time, for days, to get as thin as that.

How much longer now, before he died? How much more heat and thirst and pain could flesh stand?

For a little while he was almost hysterical again, and then came a time of deep calm, and a thought that was startling.

The lizard he had just killed. *It had crossed the barrier, still alive.* It had come from the Roller's side; the Roller had pulled off its legs and then tossed it contemptuously at him and it had come through the barrier. He'd thought, because the lizard was dead.

But it hadn't been dead; it had been unconscious.

A live lizard couldn't go through the barrier, but an unconscious one could. The barrier was not a barrier, then, to living flesh, but to conscious flesh. It was a *mental* projection, a *mental* hazard.

And with that thought, Carson started crawling along the barrier to make his last desperate gamble. A hope so forlorn that only a dying man would have dared try it.

No use weighing the odds of success. Not when, if he didn't try it, those odds were infinitely to zero.

He crawled along the barrier to the dune of sand, about four feet high, which he'd scooped out in trying—how many days ago?—to dig under the barrier or to reach water.

That mound was right at the barrier, its farther slope half on one side of the barrier, half on the other.

Taking with him a rock from the pile nearby, he climbed up to the top of the dune and over the top, and lay there against the barrier, his weight leaning against it so that if the barrier were taken away he'd roll on down the short slope, into the enemy territory.

He checked to be sure that the knife was safely in his rope belt, that the harpoon was in the crook of his left arm and that the twenty-foot rope fastened to it and to his wrist.

Then with his right hand he raised the rock with which he would hit himself on the head. Luck would have to be with him on that blow; it would have to be hard enough to knock him out, but not hard enough to knock him out for long.

He had a hunch that the Roller was watching him, and would see him roll down through the barrier, and come to investigate. It would think he was dead, he hoped—he thought it had probably drawn the same deduction about the nature of the barrier that he had drawn. But it would come cautiously. He would have a little time—

He struck.

Pain brought him back to consciousness. A sudden, sharp pain in his hip that was different from the throbbing pain in his head and the throbbing pain in his leg.

But he had, thinking things out before he had struck himself, anticipated that very pain, even hoped for it, and had steeled himself against awakening with a sudden movement.

He lay still, but opened his eyes just a slit, and saw

that he had guessed rightly. The Roller was coming closer. It was twenty feet away and the pain that had awakened him was the stone it had tossed to see whether he was alive or dead.

He lay still. It came closer, fifteen feet away, and stopped again. Carson scarcely breathed.

As nearly as possible, he was keeping his mind a blank, lest its telepathic ability detect consciousness in him. And with his mind blanked out that way, the impact if its thoughts upon his mind was nearly soul-shattering.

He felt sheer horror at the utter *alienness*, the *differentness* of those thoughts. Things that he felt but could not understand and could never express, because no terrestrial language had words, no terrestrial mind had images to fit them. The mind of a spider, he thought, or the mind of a praying mantis or a Martian sand-serpent, raised to intelligence and put in telepathic rapport with human minds, would be a homely familiar thing, compared to this.

He understood now that the Entity had been right: Man or Roller, and the universe was not a place that could hold them both. Farther apart than god and devil, there could never be even a balance between them.

Closer. Carson waited until it was only feet away, until its clawed tentacles reached out—

Oblivious to agony now, he sat up, raised and flung the harpoon with all the strength that remained to him. Or he thought it was all; sudden final strength flooded through him, along with a sudden forgetfulness of pain as definite as a nerve block.

As the Roller, deeply stabbed by the harpoon, rolled away, Carson tried to get to his feet to run after it. He couldn't do that; he fell, but kept crawling.

It reached the end of the rope, and he was jerked forward by the pull on his wrist. It dragged him a few feet and then stopped. Carson kept on going, pulling himself toward it hand over hand along the rope.

It stopped there, writhing tentacles trying in vain to pull out the harpoon. It seemed to shudder and quiver, and then it must have realized that it couldn't get away, for it rolled back toward him, clawed tentacles reaching out.

Stone knife in hand, he met it. He stabbed, again and

again, while those horrid claws ripped skin and flesh and muscle from his body.

He stabbed and slashed, and at last it was still.

A bell was ringing, and it took him a while after he'd opened his eyes to tell where he was and what it was. He was strapped into the seat of his scouter, and the visiplate before him showed only empty space. No Outsider ship and no impossible planet.

The bell was the communications plate signal; someone wanted him to switch power into the receiver. Purely reflex action enabled him to reach forward and throw the lever.

The face of Brander, captain of the *Magellan,* mothership of his group of scouters, flashed into the screen. His face was pale and his black eyes glowing with excitement.

"Magellan to Carson," he snapped. "Come on in. The fight's over. We've won!"

The screen went blank; Brander would be signaling the other scouters of his command.

Slowly, Carson set the controls for the return. Slowly, unbelievingly, he unstrapped himself from the seat and went back to get a drink at the cold-water tank. For some reason, he was unbelievably thirsty. He drank six glasses.

He leaned there against the wall, trying to think.

Had it happened? He was in good health, sound, uninjured. His thirst had been mental rather than physical; his throat hadn't been dry. His leg—

He pulled up his trouser leg and looked at the calf. There was a long white scar there, but a perfectly healed scar. It hadn't been there before. He zipped open the front of his shirt and saw that his chest and abdomen were criss-crossed with tiny, almost unnoticeable, perfectly healed scars.

It *had* happened

The scouter, under automatic control, was already entering the hatch of the mother-ship. The grapples pulled it into its individual lock, and a moment later a buzzer indicated that the lock was air-filled. Carson opened the hatch and stepped outside, went through the double door of the lock.

He went right to Brander's office, went in, and saluted.

Brander still looked dizzily dazed. "Hi, Carson," he said. "What you missed! What a show!"

"What happened, sir?"

"Don't know, exactly. We fired one salvo, and their whole fleet went up in dust! Whatever it was jumped from ship to ship in a flash, even the ones we hadn't aimed at and that were out of range! The whole fleet disintegrated before our eyes, and we didn't get the paint of a single ship scratched!

"We can't even claim credit for it. Must have been some unstable component in the metal they used, and our sighting shot just set it off. Man, oh man, too bad you missed all the excitement."

Carson managed to grin. It was a sickly ghost of a grin, for it would be days before he'd be over the mental impact of his experience, but the captain wasn't watching, and didn't notice.

"Yes, sir," he said. Common sense, more than modesty, told him he'd be branded forever as the worst liar in space if he ever said any more than that. "Yes, sir, too bad I missed all the excitement."

KEEP OUT

DAPTINE is the secret of it. Adaptine, they called it first; then it got shortened to daptine. It let us adapt.

They explained it all to us when we were ten years old; I guess they thought we were too young to understand before then, although we knew a lot of it already. They told us just after we landed on Mars.

"You're *home,* children," the Head Teacher told us after we had gone into the glassite dome they'd built for us there. And he told us there'd be a special lecture for us that evening, an important one that we must all attend.

And that evening he told us the whole story and the whys and wherefores. He stood up before us. He had to wear a heated spacesuit and helmet, of course, because the temperature in the dome was comfortable for us but already freezing cold for him and the air was already too thin for him to breathe. His voice came to us by radio from inside his helmet.

"Children," he said, "you are home. This is Mars, the planet on which you will spend the rest of your lives. You are Martians, the first Martians. You have lived five years on Earth and another five in space. Now you will spend ten years, until you are adults, in this dome, although toward the end of that time you will be allowed to spend increasingly long periods outdoors.

"Then you will go forth and make your own homes, live your own lives, as Martians. You will intermarry and your children will breed true. They too will be Martians.

"It is time you were told the history of this great experiment of which each of you is a part."

Then he told us.

Man, he said, had first reached Mars in 1985. It had been uninhabited by intelligent life (there is plenty of plant life and a few varieties of non-flying insects) and he had found it by terrestrial standards uninhabitable. Man could survive on Mars only by living inside glassite domes and wearing space suits when he went outside of them. Except by day in the warmer seasons it was too cold for him. The air was too thin for him to breathe and long exposure to sunlight—less filtered of rays harmful to him than on Earth because of the lesser atmosphere—could kill him. The plants were chemically alien to him and he could not eat them; he had to bring all his food from Earth or grow it in hydroponic tanks.

For fifty years he had tried to colonize Mars and all his efforts had failed. Besides this dome which had been built for us there was only one other outpost, another glassite dome much smaller and less than a mile away.

It had looked as though mankind could never spread to the other planets of the solar system besides Earth for of all them Mars was the least inhospitable; if he couldn't live here there was no use even trying to colonize the others.

And then, in 2034, thirty years ago, a brilliant biochemist named Waymoth had discovered daptine. A miracle drug that worked not on the animal or person to whom it was given but on the progeny he conceived during a limited period of time after inoculation.

It gave his progeny almost limitless adaptability to changing conditions, provided the changes were made gradually.

Dr. Waymoth had inoculated and then mated a pair of guinea pigs; they had borne a litter of five and by placing each member of the litter under different and gradually changing conditions, he had obtained amazing results. When they attained maturity one of those guinea pigs was living comfortably at a temperature of forty below zero Fahrenheit, another was quite happy at a hundred and fifty above. A third was thriving on a diet that would have been deadly poison for an ordinary animal and a fourth was contented under a constant X-ray bombardment that would have killed one of its parents within minutes.

Subsequent experiments with many litters showed that

animals who had been adapted to similar conditions bred true and their progeny was conditioned from birth to live under those conditions.

"Ten years later, ten years ago," the Head Teacher told us, "you children were born. Born of parents carefully selected from those who volunteered for the experiment. And from birth you have been brought up under carefully controlled and gradually changing conditions.

"From the time you were born the air you have breathed has been very gradually thinned and its oxygen content reduced. Your lungs have compensated by becoming much greater in capacity, which is why your chests are so much larger than those of your teachers and attendants; when you are fully mature and are breathing air like that of Mars, the difference will be even greater.

"Your bodies are growing fur to enable you to stand the increasing cold. You are comfortable now under conditions which would kill ordinary people quickly. Since you were four years old your nurses and teachers have had to wear special protection to survive conditions that seem normal to you.

"In another ten years, at maturity, you will be completely acclimated to Mars. Its air will be your air; its food plants your food. Its extremes of temperature will be easy for you to endure and its median temperatures pleasant to you. Already, because of the five years we spent in space under gradually decreased gravitational pull, the gravity of Mars seems normal to you.

"It will be your planet, to live on and to populate. You are the children of Earth but you are the first Martians."

Of course we had known a lot of those things already.

The last year was the best. By then the air inside the dome—except for the pressurized parts where our teachers and attendants live—was almost like that outside, and we were allowed out for increasingly long periods. It is good to be in the open.

The last few months they relaxed segregation of the sexes so we could begin choosing mates, although they told us there is to be no marriage until after the final day, after our full clearance. Choosing was not difficult in my case. I had made my choice long since and I'd felt sure that she felt the same way; I was right.

Tomorrow is the day of our freedom. Tomorrow we will be Martians, *the* Martians. Tomorrow we shall take over the planet.

Some among us are impatient, have been impatient for weeks now, but wiser counsel prevailed and we are waiting. We have waited twenty years and we can wait until the final day.

And tomorrow is the final day.

Tomorrow, at a signal, we will kill the teachers and the other Earthmen among us before we go forth. They do not suspect, so it will be easy.

We have dissimilated for years now, and they do not know how we hate them. They do not know how disgusting and hideous we find them, with their ugly misshapen bodies, so narrow shouldered and tiny chested, their weak sibilant voices that need amplification to carry in our Martian air, and above all their white pasty hairless skins.

We shall kill them and then we shall go and smash the other dome so all the Earthmen there will die too.

If more Earthmen ever come to punish us, we can live and hide in the hills where they'll never find us. And if they try to build more domes here we'll smash them. We want no more to do with Earth.

This is our planet and we want no aliens. Keep off!

FIRST TIME MACHINE

DR. GRAINGER said solemnly, "Gentlemen, the first time machine."

His three friends stared at it.

It was a box about six inches square, with dials and a switch.

"You need only to hold it in your hand," said Dr. Grainger, "set the dials for the date you want, press the button—and you are there."

Smedley, one of the doctor's three friends, reached for the box, held it and studied it. "Does it really work?"

"I tested it briefly," said the doctor. "I set it one day back and pushed the button. Saw myself—my own back—just walking out of the room. Gave me a bit of a turn."

"What would have happened if you'd rushed to the door and kicked yourself in the seat of the pants?"

Dr. Grainger laughed. "Maybe I couldn't have—because it would have changed the past. That's the old paradox of time travel, you know. What would happen if one went back in time and killed one's own grandfather before he met one's grandmother?"

Smedley, the box still in his hand, suddenly was backing away from the three other men. He grinned at them. "That," he said, "is just what I'm going to do. I've been setting the date dials sixty years back while you've been talking."

"Smedley! Don't!" Dr. Grainger started forward.

"Stop, Doc. Or I'll press the button now. Otherwise I'll explain to you." Grainger stopped. "I've heard of that paradox too. And it's always interested me because I knew I *would* kill my grandfather if I ever had a chance to. I hated him. He was a cruel bully, made life a hell for my grandmother and my parents. So this is a chance I've been waiting for."

Smedley's hand reached for the button and pressed it.

There was a sudden blur . . . Smedley was standing in a field. It took him only a moment to orient himself. If this spot was where Dr. Grainger's house would some day be built, then his great-grandfather's farm would be only a mile south. He started walking. En route he found a piece of wood that made a fine club.

Near the farm, he saw a red-headed young man beating a dog with a whip.

"Stop that!" Smedley yelled, rushing up.

"Mind your own damn business," said the young man as he lashed with the whip again.

Smedley swung the club.

Sixty years later, Dr. Grainger said solemnly, "Gentlemen, the first time machine."

His two friends stared at it.

AND THE GODS
LAUGHED

Y OU know how it is when you're with a work crew on one of the asteroids. You're there, stuck for the month you signed up for, with four other guys and nothing to do but talk. Space on the little tugs that you go in and return in, and live in while you're there, is at such a premium that there isn't room for a book or a magazine nor equipment for games. And you're out of radio range except for the usual once-a-terrestrial-day, system-wide newscasts.

So talking is the only indoor sport you can go in for. Talking and listening. You've plenty of time for both because a work-day, in space-suits, is only four hours and that with four fifteen-minute back-to-the-ship rests.

Anyway, what I'm trying to say is that talk is cheap on one of those work crews. With most of the day to do nothing else, you listen to some real whoppers, stories that would make the old-time Liars Club back on Earth seem like Sunday-school meetings. And if your mind runs that way, you've got plenty of time to think up some yourself.

Charlie Dean was on our crew, and Charlie could tell some dillies. He'd been on Mars back in the old days when there was still trouble with the *bolies,* and when living on Mars was a lot like living on Earth back in the days of Indian fighting. The *bolies* thought and fought a lot like Amerinds, even though they were quadrupeds that looked like alligators on stilts—if you can picture an alligator on stilts—and used blow-guns instead of bows and arrows. Or was it crossbows that the Amerinds used against the colonists?

Anyway, Charlie's just finished a whopper that was really too good for the first tryout of the trip. We'd just landed, you see, and were resting up from doing nothing en route, and usually the yarns start off easy and believable and don't work up to real depth-of-space lying until along about the fourth week when everybody's bored stiff.

"So we took this head *bolie*," Charlie was ending up, "and you know what kind of flappy little ears they've got, and we put a couple of zircon-studded earrings in its ears and let it go, and back it went to the others, and then darned if—" Well, I won't go on with Charlie's yarn, because it hasn't got anything to do with his story except that it brought earrings into the conversation.

Blake shook his head gloomily and then turned to me. He said, "Hank, what went on on Ganymede? You were on that ship that went out there a few months ago, weren't you—the first one that got through? I've never read or heard much about that trip."

"Me either," Charlie said. "Except that the Ganymedeans turned out to be humanoid beings about four feet tall and didn't wear a thing except earrings. Kind of immodest, wasn't it?"

I grinned. "You wouldn't have thought so if you'd seen the Ganymedeans. With them, it didn't matter. Anyway, they didn't wear earrings."

"You're crazy," Charlie said. "Sure, I know you were on that expedition and I wasn't, but you're still crazy, because I had a quick look at some of the pictures they brought back. The natives wore earrings."

"No," I said. "Earrings wore *them.*"

Blake sighed deeply. "I knew it, I knew it," he said. "There was something wrong with this trip from the start. Charlie pops off the first day with a yarn that should have been worked up to gradually. And now you say—Or is there something wrong with my *sense of earring?*"

I chuckled. "Not a thing, Skipper."

Charlie said, "I've heard of men biting dogs, but earrings wearing people is a new one. Hank, I hate to say it—but just consider it said."

Anyway, I had their attention. And now was as good a time as any.

I said, "If you read about the trip, you know we left Earth about eight months ago, for a six-months' round trip. There were six of us in the M-94; me and two others made up the crew and there were three specialists to do the studying and exploring. Not the really top-flight specialists, though, because the trip was too risky to send them. That was the third ship to try for Ganymede and the other two had cracked up on outer Jovian satellites that the observatories hadn't spotted from Earth because they are too small to show up in the scopes at that distance.

"When you get there you find there's practically an asteroid belt around Jupiter, most of them so black they don't reflect light to speak of and you can't see them till they hit you or you hit them. But most of them—"

"Skip the satellites," Blake interrupted, "unless they wore earrings."

"Or unless earrings wore *them,*" said Charlie.

"Neither," I admitted. "All right, so we were lucky and got through the belt. And landed. Like I said, there were six of us. Lecky, the biologist. Haynes geologist and mineralogist. And Hilda Race, who loved little flowers and was a botanist, egad! You'd have loved Hilda—at a distance. Somebody must have wanted to get rid of her, and sent her on that trip. She gushed; you know the type.

"And then there was Art Willis and Dick Carney. They gave Dick skipper's rating for the trip; he knew enough astrogation to get us through. So Dick was skipper and Art and I were flunkies and gunmen. Our main job was to go along with the specialists whenever they left the ship and stand guard over them against whatever dangers might pop up."

"And did anything pop?" Charlie demanded.

"I'm coming to that," I told him. "We found Ganymede not so bad, as places go. Gravity low, of course, but you could get around easily and keep your balance once you got used to it. And the air was breathable for a couple of hours; after that you found yourself panting like a dog.

"Lot of funny animals, but none of them were very dangerous. No reptilian life; all of it mammalian, but a funny kind of mammalian if you know what I mean."

Blake said, "I don't want to know what you mean. Get to the natives and the earrings."

I said, "But of course with animals like that, you never *know* whether they're dangerous until you've been around them for a while. You can't judge by size or looks. Like if you'd never seen a snake, you'd never guess that a little coral snake was dangerous, would you? And a Martian zeezee looks for all the world like an overgrown guinea-pig. But without a gun—or with one, for that matter—I'd rather face a grizzly bear or a—"

"The earrings," said Blake. "You were talking about earrings."

I said, "Oh, yes; earrings. Well, the natives wore them —for now, I'll put it that way, to make it easier to tell. One earring apiece, even though they had two ears. Gave them a sort of lopsided look, because they were pretty fair-sized earrings—like hoops of plain gold, two or three inches in diameter.

"Anyway, the tribe we landed near wore them that way. We could see the village—a very primitive sort of place made of mud huts—from where we landed. We had a council of war and decided that three of us would stay in the ship and the other three go to the village. Lecky, the biologist, and Art Willis and I with guns. We didn't know what we might run into, see? And Lecky was chosen because he was pretty much of a linguist. He had a flair for languages and could talk them almost as soon as he heard them.

"They'd heard us land and a bunch of them—about forty, I guess—met us half-way between the ship and the village. And they were friendly. Funny people. Quiet and dignified and acting not at all like you'd expect savages to act toward people landing out of the sky. You know how most primitives react—either they practically worship you or else they try to kill you.

"We went to the village with them—and there were about forty more of them there; they'd split forces just as we did, for the reception committee. Another sign of intelligence. They recognized Lecky as leader, and started jabbering to him in a lingo that sounded more like a pig grunting than a man talking. And pretty soon Lecky was making an experimental grunt or two in return.

"Everything seemed on the up and up, and no danger. And they weren't paying much attention to Art and me, so we decided to wander off for a stroll around the village to see what the country was like and whether there were any dangerous beasties or what-not. We didn't see any

animals, but we did see another native. He acted different
from the others—very different. He threw a spear at us
and then ran. And it was Art who noticed that this native
didn't wear an earring.

"And then breathing began to get a bit hard for us—
we'd been away from the ship over an hour—so we went
back to the village to collect Lecky and take him to the
ship. He was getting along so well that he hated to leave,
but he was starting to pant, too, so we talked him into it.
He was wearing one of the earrings, and said they'd given
it to him as a present, and he'd made them a return present
of a pocket slide-rule he happened to have with him.

" 'Why a slide-rule?' I asked him. 'Those things cost
money and we've got plenty of junk that would make them
happier.'

" 'That's what you think,' he said. 'They figured out how
to multiply and divide with it almost as soon as I showed
it to them. I showed them how to extract square roots,
and I was starting on cube roots when you fellows came
back.'

"I whistled and took a close look to see if maybe he was
kidding me. He didn't seem to be. But I noticed that he
was walking strangely and—well, acting just a bit strangely,
somehow, although I couldn't put my finger on what it
was. I decided finally that he was just a bit over-excited.
This was Lecky's first trip off Earth, so that was natural
enough.

"Inside the ship, as soon as Lecky got his breath back—
the last hundred yards pretty well winded us—he started
in to tell Haynes and Hilda Race about the Ganymedeans.
Most of it was too technical for me, but I got that they had
some strange contradictions in them. As far as their way of
life was concerned, they were more primitive than Australian bushmen. But they had brains and a philosophy
and a knowledge of mathematics and pure science. They'd
told him some things about atomic structure that excited
hell out of him. He was in a dither to get back to Earth
where he could get at equipment to check some of those
things.

"And he said the earring was a sign of membership in
the tribe—they'd acknowledged him as a friend and com-
patriot and what-not by giving it to him."

Blake asked, "Was it gold?"

"I'm coming to that," I told him. I was feeling cramped from sitting so long in one position on the bunk, and I stood up and stretched.

There isn't much room to stretch in an asteroid tug and my hand hit against the pistol resting in the clips on the wall. I said, "What's the pistol for, Blake?"

He shrugged. "Rules. Has to be one hand weapon on every space-craft. Heaven knows why, on an asteroid ship. Unless the council thinks some day an asteroid may get mad at us when we tow it out of orbit so it cracks up another. Say, did I even tell you about the time we had a little twenty-ton rock in tow and—"

"Shut up Blake," Charlie said. "He's just getting to those damn earrings."

"Yeah, the earrings," I said. I took the pistol down from the wall and looked at it. It was an old-fashioned metal project weapon, twenty-shot, circa 2000. It was loaded and usable, but dirty. It hurts me to see a dirty gun.

I went on talking, but I sat back down on the bunk, took an old handkerchief out of my duffle-box and started to clean and polish the hand-gun while I talked.

I said, "He wouldn't let us take the earring off. Acted just a little funny about it when Haynes wanted to analyze the metal. Told Haynes he could get one of his own if he wanted to mess with it. And then he went back to rhapsodizing over the superior knowledge the Ganymedeans had shown.

"Next day all of them wanted to go to the village, but we'd made the rule that not more than three of the six of us would be outside the ship at once, and they'd have to take turns. Since Lecky could talk their grunt-lingo, he and Hilda went first, and Art went along to guard them. Looked safe enough to work that proportion now—two scientists to one guard. Outside of that one native that had thrown a spear at Art and me, there hadn't been a sign of danger. And he'd looked like a half-wit and missed us by twenty feet anyway. We hadn't even bothered to shoot at him.

"They were back, panting for breath, in less than two hours. Hilda Race's eyes were shining and she was wearing one of the rings in her left ear. She looked as proud as though it was a royal crown making her queen of Mars or something. She gushed about it, as soon as she got her wind back and stopped panting.

"I went on the next trip, with Lecky and Haynes.

"Haynes was kind of grumpy, for some reason, and said they weren't going to put one of those rings in his ear, even if he did want one for analysis. They could just hand it to him, or else.

"Again nobody paid much attention to me after we got there, and I wandered around the village. I was on the outskirts of it when I heard a yell—and I ran back to the center of town but fast, because it sounded like Haynes.

"There was a crowd around a spot in the middle of— well, call it the compound. Took me a minute to wedge my way through, scattering natives to all sides as I went. And when I got to the middle of things, Haynes was just getting up, and there was a big stain of red on the front of his white linen coat.

"I grabbed him to help him up, and said, 'Haynes, what's the matter? You hurt?'

"He shook his head slowly, as though he was kind of dazed, and then he said, 'I'm all right, Hank. I'm all right. I just stumbled and fell.' Then he saw me looking at that red stain, and smiled. I guess it was a smile, but it didn't look natural. He said, 'That's not blood, Hank. Some native red wine I happened to spill. Part of the ceremony.'

"I started to ask what ceremony, and then I saw he was wearing one of the gold earrings. I thought that was damn funny, but he started talking to Lecky, and he looked and acted all right—well, fairly all right. Lecky was telling him what a few of the grunts meant, and he acted awful interested—but somehow I got the idea he was pretending most of that interest so he wouldn't have to talk to me. He acted as though he was thinking hard, inside, and maybe he was making up a better story to cover that stain on his clothes and the fact that he'd changed his mind so quick about the earring.

"I was getting the notion that something was rotten in the state of Ganymede, but I didn't know what. I decided to keep my yap shut and my eyes open till I found out.

"I'd have plenty of time to study Haynes later, though, so I wandered off again to the edge of the village and just outside it. And it occurred to me that if there was anything I wasn't supposed to see, I might stand a better chance of seeing it if I got under cover. There were plenty of bushes around and I picked out a good clump of them and hid. From the way my lungs worked, I figured I had maybe a half hour before we'd have to start back for the ship.

"And less than half that time had gone by before I saw something."

I stopped talking to hold the pistol up to the light and squint through the barrel. It was getting pretty clean, but there were a couple of spots left up near the muzzle end.

Blake said, "Let me guess. You saw a Martian traag-hound standing on his tail, sing Annie Laurie."

"Worse than that," I said. "I saw one of those Ganymede natives get his legs bit off. And it annoyed him."

"It would annoy anyone," said Blake. "Even me, and I'm a pretty mild-tempered guy. What bit them off?"

"I never found out," I told him. "It was something under water. There was a stream there, going by the village, and there must have been something like crocodiles in it. Two natives came out of the village and started to wade across the stream. About half-way over one of them gave a yelp and went down.

"The other grabbed him and pulled him up on the other bank. And both his legs were gone just above the knees.

"And the damnedest thing happened. The native with his legs off stood up on the stumps of them and started talking—or grunting—quite calmly to his companion, who grunted back. And if tone of voice meant anything, he was annoyed. Nothing more. He tried walking on the stumps of his legs, and found he couldn't go very fast.

"And then he gave a gesture that looked for all the world like a shrug, and reached up and took off his earring and held it out to the other native. And then came the strangest part.

"The other native took it—*and the very instant the ring left the hand of the first one*—the one with his legs off— *he fell down dead*. The other one picked up the corpse and threw it in the water, and went on.

"And as soon as he was out of sight I went back to get Lecky and Haynes and take them to the ship. They were ready to leave when I got there.

"I thought I was worried a bit, but I hadn't seen anything yet. Not till I started back to the ship with Lecky and Haynes. Haynes, first thing I noticed, had the stain gone from the front of his coat. Wine or—whatever it was— somebody'd managed to get it out for him, and the coat wasn't even wet. But it was torn, pierced. I hadn't noticed that before. But there was a place there that looked like a spear had gone through his coat.

"And then he happened to get in front of me, and I saw that there was another tear or rip just like it *in back* of his coat. Taken together, it was like somebody'd pushed a spear through him, from front to back. When he'd yelled.

"But if a spear'd gone through him like that, then he was dead. And there he was walking ahead of me back to the ship. With one of those earrings in his left ear—and I couldn't help but remember about that native and the thing in the river. That native was sure enough dead, too, with his legs off like that, but he hadn't found it out until he'd handed that earring away.

"I can tell you I was plenty thoughtful that evening, watching everybody, and it seemed to me that they were all acting strange. Especially Hilda—you'd have to watch a hippopotamus acting kittenish to get an idea. Haynes and Lecky seemed thoughtful and subdued, like they were planning something, maybe. After a while Art came up from the glory hole and he was wearing one of those rings.

"Gave me a kind of shiver to realize that—if what I was thinking could possibly be true—then there was only me and Dick left. And I'd better start comparing notes with Dick pretty soon. He was working on a report, but I knew pretty soon he'd make his routine inspection trip through the storerooms before turning in, and I'd corner him then.

"Meanwhile, I watched the other four and I got surer and surer. And more and more scared. They were trying their darnedest to act natural, but once in a while one of them would slip. For one thing, they'd *forget to talk*. I mean, one of them would turn to another as though he was saying something, but he wouldn't. And then, as though remembering, he'd start in the middle of it—like he'd been talking without words before, telepathically.

"And pretty soon Dick gets up and goes out, and I followed him. We got to one of the side storerooms and I

closed the door. 'Dick,' I asked, 'have you noticed it?' And
he wanted to know what I was talking about.

"So I told him. I said, 'Those four people out there—
they *aren't the ones we started with*. What happened to
Art and Hilda and Lecky and Haynes? What the hell goes
on here? Haven't you noticed *anything* out of the ordinary?'

"And Dick sighed, kind of, and said, 'Well, it didn't
work. We need more practice, then. Come on and we'll
tell you all about it.' And he opened the door and held out
his hand to me—and the sleeve of his shirt pulled back a
little from the wrist and he was wearing one of those gold
things, like the others, only he was wearing it as a bracelet
instead of an earring.

"I—well, I was too dumbfounded to say anything. I
didn't take the hand he held out, but I followed him back
into the main room. And then—while Lecky, who seemed
to be the leader, I think—held a gun on me, they told me
about it.

"And it was even screwier, and worse, than I'd dare
guess.

"They didn't have any name for themselves, because
they had no language—what you'd really call a spoken
or written language—of their own. You see, they were
telepathic, and you don't need a language for that. If you
tried to translate their thought for themselves, the nearest
word you could find for it would be "we"—the first person
plural pronoun. Individually, they identified themselves to
one another by numbers rather than names.

"And just as they had no language of their own, they
had no real bodies of their own, nor active minds of their
own. They were parasitic in a sense that earthmen can't
conceive. They were *entities*, apart from— Well, it's difficult to explain, but in a way they had no real existence
when not attached to a body they could animate and *think
with*. The easiest way to put it is that a detached—uh—
earring god, which is what the Ganymedean natives called
them—was asleep, dormant, ineffective. Had no power of
thought or motion in itself."

Charlie and Blake were looking bewildered. Charlie said,
"You're trying to say, Hank, that when one of them came
in contact with a person, they took over that person and
ran him and thought with his mind but—uh—kept their

own identity? And what happened to the person they took over?"

I said, "As near as I could make out, he stayed there, too, as it were, but was dominated by the entity. I mean, there remained all his memories, and his individuality, but something else was in the driver's seat. Running him. Didn't matter whether he was alive or dead, either, as long as his body wasn't in too bad shape. Like Haynes— they'd had to kill him to put an earring on him. He was dead, in that if that ring was removed, he'd have fallen flat and never got up again, unless it was put back.

"Like the native whose legs had been cut off. The entity running him had decided the body was no longer practicable for use, so he handed himself back to the other native, see? And they'd find another body in better shape for him to use.

"They didn't tell me where they came from, except that it was outside the solar system, nor just how they got to Ganymede. Not by themselves, though, because they couldn't even exist by themselves. They must have got as far as Ganymede as parasites of visitors that had landed there at some time or other. Maybe millions of years ago. And they couldn't get off Ganymede, of course, till we landed there. Space travel hadn't developed on Ganymede—"

Charlie interrupted me again, "But if they were so smart, why didn't they develop it themselves?"

"They couldn't," I told him. "They weren't any smarter than the minds they occupied. Well, a little smarter, in a way, because they could use those minds to their full capacity and people—Terrestrial or Ganymedean—don't do that. But even the full capacity of the mind of a Ganymedean savage wasn't sufficient to develop a space-ship.

"But now they had *us*—I mean, they had Lecky and Haynes and Hilda and Art and Dick—and they had our space-ship, and they were going to Earth, because they knew all about it and about conditions there from our minds. They planned, simply, to take over Earth and—uh— *run* it. They didn't explain the details of how they propagate, but I gathered that there wouldn't be any shortage of earrings to go around, on Earth. Earrings or bracelets or, however they'd attach themselves.

"Bracelets, probably, or arm or leg bands, because wearing earrings like that would be too conspicuous on Earth, and they'd have to work in secret for a while. Take over a few people at a time, without letting the others know what was going on.

"And Lecky—or the thing that was running Lecky—told me they'd been using me as a guinea pig, that they could have put a ring on me, taken me over, at any time. But they wanted a check on how they were doing at imitating normal people. They wanted to know whether or not I got suspicious and guessed the truth.

"So Dick—or the thing that was running him—had kept himself out of sight under Dick's sleeve, so if I got suspicious of the others, I'd talk it over with Dick—just as I really did do. And that let them know they needed a lot more practice animating those bodies before they took the ship back to Earth to start their campaign there.

"And, well, that was the whole story and they told it to me to watch my reactions, as a normal human. And then Lecky took a ring out of his pocket and held it out toward me with one hand, keeping the pistol on me with the other hand.

"He told me I might as well put it on because if I didn't, he could shoot me first and then put it on me—but that they greatly preferred to take over undamaged bodies and that it would be better for me, too, if I—that is, my body—didn't die first.

"But naturally, I didn't see it that way. I pretended to reach out for the ring, hesitantly, but instead I batted the gun out of his hand, and made a dive for it as it hit the floor.

"I got it, too, just as they all came for me. And I fired three shots into them before I saw that it wasn't even annoying them. The only way you can stop a body animated by one of those rings is to fix it so it can't move, like cutting off the legs or something. A bullet in the heart doesn't worry it.

"But I'd backed to the door and got out of it—out into the Gandymedean night, without even a coat on. It was colder than hell, too. And after I got out there, there just wasn't any place to go. Except back in the ship, and I wasn't going there.

"They didn't come out after me—didn't bother to. They knew that within three hours—four at the outside—I'd be unconscious from insufficient oxygen. If the cold, or something else, didn't get me first.

"Maybe there was some way out, but I didn't see one. I just sat down on a stone about a hundred yards from the ship and tried to think of something I could do. But—"

I didn't go anywhere with the "but—" and there was a moment's silence, and then Charlie said, "Well?"

And Blake said, "What did you do?"

"Nothing," I said. "I couldn't think of a thing to do. I just sat there."

"Till morning?"

"No. I lost consciousness before morning. I came to while it was still dark, in the ship."

Blake was looking at me with a puzzled frown. He said, "The hell. You mean—"

And then Charlie let out a sudden yip and dived head-first out of the bunk he'd been lying on, and grabbed the gun out of my hand. I'd just finished cleaning it and slipped the cartridge-clip back in.

And then, with it in his hand, he stood there staring at me as though he'd never seen me before.

Blake said, "Sit down, Charlie. Don't you know when you're being ribbed? But—uh—better keep the gun, just the same."

Charlie kept the gun all right, and turned it around to point at me. He said, "I'm making a damn fool out of myself all right, but—Hank, *roll up your sleeves.*"

I grinned and stood up. I said, "Don't forget my ankles, too."

But there was something dead serious in his face, and I didn't push him too far. Blake said, "He could even have it on him somewhere else, with adhesive tape. I mean on the million-to-one chance that he wasn't kidding."

Charlie nodded without turning to look at Blake. He said, "Hank, I hate to ask it, but—"

I sighed, and then chuckled. I said, "Well, I was just going to take a shower anyway."

It was hot in the ship, and I was wearing only shoes and a pair of coveralls. Paying no attention to Blake and Charlie, I slipped them off and stepped through the oilsilk curtains of the little shower cubicle. And turned on the water.

Over the sound of the shower, I could hear Blake laughing and Charlie cursing softly to himself.

And when I came out of the shower, drying myself, even Charlie was grinning. Blake said, "And I thought that yarn Charlie just told was a dilly. This trip is backwards; we'll end up having to tell each other the truth."

There was a sharp rapping on the hull beside the airlock, and Charlie Dean went to open it. He growled, "If you tell Zeb and Ray what chumps you made out of us, I'll beat your damn ears in. You and your earring gods . . ."

Portion of telepathic report of No. 67843, on Asteroid— J-864A to No. 5463, on Terra:

"As planned, I tested credulity of terrestrial minds by telling them the true story of what happened on Ganymede.

Found them capable of acceptance thereof.

This proves that our idea of embedding ourselves within the flesh of these terrestrial creatures was an excellent one and is essential to the success of our plan. True, this is less simple than our method on Ganymede, but we must continue to perform the operation upon each terrestrial being as we take him over. Bracelets or other appendages would arouse suspicion.

There is no necessity in wasting a month here. I shall now take command of the ship and return. We will report no ore present here. The four of us who will animate the four terrestrials now aboard this ship will report to you from Terra . . ."

THE WEAPON

THE ROOM was quiet in the dimness of early evening. Dr. James Graham, key scientist of a very important project, sat in his favorite chair, thinking. It was so still that he could hear the turning of pages in the next room as his son leafed through a picture book.

Often Graham did his best work, his most creative thinking, under these circumstances, sitting alone in an unlighted room in his own apartment after the day's regular work. But tonight his mind would not work constructively. Mostly he thought about his mentally arrested son—his only son —in the next room. The thoughts were loving thoughts, not the bitter anguish he had felt years ago when he had first learned of the boy's condition. The boy was happy; wasn't that the main thing? And to how many men is given a child who will always be a child, who will not grow up to leave him? Certainly that was rationalization, but what is wrong with rationalization when— The doorbell rang.

Graham rose and turned on lights in the almost-dark room before he went through the hallway to the door. He was not annoyed; tonight, at this moment, almost any interruption to his thoughts was welcome.

He opened the door. A stranger stood there; he said, "Dr. Graham? My name is Niemand; I'd like to talk to you. May I come in a moment?"

Graham looked at him. He was a small man, nondescript, obviously harmless—possibly a reporter or an insurance agent.

But it didn't matter what he was. Graham found himself saying, "Of course. Come in, Mr. Niemand." A few minutes of conversation, he justified himself by thinking, might divert his thoughts and clear his mind.

"Sit down," he said, in the living room. "Care for a drink?"

Niemand said, "No, thank you." He sat in the chair; Graham sat on the sofa.

The small man interlocked his fingers; he leaned forward. He said, "Dr. Graham, you are the man whose scientific work is more likely than that of any other man to end the human race's chance for survival."

A crackpot, Graham thought. Too late now he realized that he should have asked the man's business before admitting him. It would be an embarrassing interview; he disliked being rude, yet only rudeness was effective.

"Dr. Graham, the weapon on which you are working—"

The visitor stopped and turned his head as the door that led to a bedroom opened and a boy of fifteen came in. The boy didn't notice Niemand; he ran to Graham.

"Daddy, will you read to me now?" The boy of fifteen laughed the sweet laughter of a child of four.

Graham put an arm around the boy. He looked at his visitor, wondering whether he had known about the boy. From the lack of surprise on Niemand's face, Graham felt sure he had known.

"Harry"—Graham's voice was warm with affection—"Daddy's busy. Just for a little while. Go back to your room; I'll come and read to you soon."

" 'Chicken Little'? You'll read me 'Chicken Little'?"

"If you wish. Now run along. Wait. Harry, this is Mr. Niemand."

The boy smiled bashfully at the visitor. Niemand said, "Hi, Harry," and smiled back at him, holding out his hand. Graham, watching, was sure now that Niemand had known; the smile and the gesture were for the boy's mental age, not his physical one.

The boy took Niemand's hand. For a moment it seemed that he was going to climb into Niemand's lap, and Graham pulled him back gently. He said, "Go to your room now, Harry."

The boy skipped back into his bedroom, not closing the door.

Niemand's eyes met Graham's and he said, "I like him," with obvious sincerity. He added, "I hope that what you're going to read to him will always be true."

Graham didn't understand. Niemand said, " 'Chicken Little,' I mean. It's a fine story—but may 'Chicken Little' always be wrong about the sky falling down."

Graham suddenly had liked Niemand when Niemand had shown liking for the boy. Now he remembered that he must close the interview quickly. He rose, in dismissal. He said, "I fear you're wasting your time and mine, Mr. Niemand. I know all the arguments, everything you can say I've heard a thousand times. Possibly there is truth in what you believe, but it does not concern me. I'm a scientist, and only a scientist. Yes, it is public knowledge that I am working on a weapon, a rather ultimate one. But, for me personally, that is only a by-product of the fact that I am advancing science. I have thought it through, and I have found that that is my only concern."

"But, Dr. Graham, is humanity *ready* for an ultimate weapon?"

Graham frowned. "I have told you my point of view, Mr. Niemand."

Niemand rose slowly from the chair. He said, "Very well, if you do not choose to discuss it, I'll say no more." He passed a hand across his forehead. "I'll leave, Dr. Graham. I wonder, though . . . may I change my mind about the drink you offered me?"

Graham's irritation faded. He said, "Certainly. Will whisky and water do?"

"Admirably."

Graham excused himself and went into the kitchen. He got the decanter of whisky, another of water, ice cubes, glasses.

When he returned to the living room, Niemand was just leaving the boy's bedroom. He heard Niemand's "Good night, Harry," and Harry's happy " 'Night, Mr. Niemand."

Graham made drinks. A little later, Niemand declined a second one and started to leave.

Niemand said, "I took the liberty of bringing a small gift to your son, doctor. I gave it to him while you were getting the drinks for us. I hope you'll forgive me."

"Of course. Thank you. Good night."

Graham closed the door; he walked through the living room into Harry's room. He said, "All right, Harry. Now I'll read to—"

There was sudden sweat on his forehead, but he forced his face and his voice to be calm as he stepped to the side of the bed. "May I see that, Harry?" When he had it safely, his hands shook as he examined it.

He thought, *only a madman would give a loaded revolver to an idiot.*

A WORD
FROM OUR SPONSOR

Looking at it one way, you could say that it happened a great many different times over a twenty-four hour period; another way, that it happened once and all at once.

It happened, that is, at 8:30 P.M. on Wednesday, June 9th, 1954. That means it came first, of course, in the Marshall Islands, the Gilbert Islands and in all the other islands —and on all the ships at sea—which were just west of the International Date Line. It was twenty-four hours later in happening in the various islands and on the various ships just east of the International Date Line.

Of course, on ships which, during that twenty-four hour period, crossed the date line from east to west and therefore had two 8:30 P.M.'s, both on June 9th, it happened twice. On ships crossing the other way and therefore having *no* 8:30 P.M. (or one bell, if we must be nautical) it didn't happen at all.

That may sound complicated, but it's simple, really. Just say that it happened at 8:30 P.M. everywhere, regardless of time belts and strictly in accordance with whether or not the area in question had or did not have daylight saving time. Simply that: 8:30 P.M. *everywhere*.

And 8:30 P.M. everywhere is just about the optimum moment for radio listening, which undoubtedly had something to do with it. Otherwise somebody or something went to an awful lot of unnecessary trouble, so to stagger the times that they would be the same all over the world.

Even if, at 8:30 on June 9, 1954, you weren't listening to your radio—and you probably were—you certainly remember it. The world was on the brink of war. Oh, it had been on the brink of war for years, but this time its toes were over the edge and it balanced precariously. There were special sessions in—but we'll come to that later.

Take Dan Murphy, inebriated Australian of Irish birth, being pugnacious in a Brisbane pub. And the Dutchman known as Dutch being pugnacious right back. The radio blaring. The bartender trying to quiet them down and the rest of the crowd trying to egg them on. You've seen it happen and you've heard it happen, unless you make a habit of staying out of waterfront saloons.

Murphy had stepped back from the bar already and was wiping his hands on the sides of his dirty sweat shirt. He was well into the preliminaries. He said, "Why, you —— —— —— — ——!" and waited for the riposte. He wasn't disappointed. "—— you!" said Dutch.

That, as it happened, was at twenty-nine minutes and twenty-eight seconds past eight o'clock, June 9, 1954. Dan Murphy took a second or two to smile happily and get his dukes up. Then something happened to the radio. For a fraction of a second, only that long, it went dead. Then a quite calm, quite ordinary voice said, "And now a word from our sponsor." And there was something—some ineffably indefinable quality—in the voice that made everybody in the room listen and hear. Dan Murphy with his right pulled back for a roundhouse swing; Dutch the Dutchman with his feet ready to step back from it and his forearm ready to block it; the bartender with his hand on the bung starter under the bar and his knees bent ready to vault over the bar.

A full frozen second, and then a different voice, also from the radio, said "Fight."

One word, only one word. Probably the only time in history that "*a* word from our sponsor" on the radio had been just that. And I won't try to describe the inflection of that word; it has been too variously described. You'll find people who swear it was said viciously, in hatred; others who are equally sure that it was calm and cold. But it was unmistakably a *command,* in whatever tone of voice.

And then there was a fraction of a second of silence again and then the regular program—in the case of the radio in the Brisbane pub, an Hawaiian instrumental group —was back on.

Dan Murphy took another step backwards and said, "Wait a minute. What the hell was that?"

Dutch the Dutchman had already lowered his big fists and was turning to the radio. Everybody else in the place was staring at it already. The bartender had taken his hand off the bung-starter. He said, "—— me for a —— ——. What was *that* an ad for?"

"Let's call this off a minute, Dutch," Dan Murphy said. "I got a funny feeling like that —— —— radio was talking to *me*. Personally. And what the —— —— —— business has a bloody wireless set got telling *me* what to do?"

"Me too," Dutch said, sincerely if a bit ambiguously. He put his elbows on the bar and stared at the radio. Nothing but the plaintive sliding wail of an Hawaiian ensemble came out of it.

Dan Murphy stepped to the bar beside him. He said, "What the devil were we fighting about?"

"You called me a —— —— —— —— ——," Dutch reminded him. "And I said, —— you."

"Oh," Murphy said. "All right, in a couple minutes I'll knock your head off. But right now I want to think a bit. How's about a drink?"

"Sure," Dutch said.

For some reason, they never got around to starting the fight.

Take, two and a half hours later (but still at 8:30 P.M.), the conversation of Mr. and Mrs. Wade Evans of Oklahoma City, presently in their room at the Grand Hotel, Singapore, dressing to go night-clubbing in what they thought was the most romantic city of their round-the-world cruise. The room radio going, but quite softly (Mrs. Evans had turned it down so her husband wouldn't miss a word of what she had to say to him, which was *plenty*).

"*And* the way you acted yesterday evening on the boat with that Miss—Mam*selle* Cartier — Cah-tee-*yay*. Half your age, and *French*. Honestly, Wade, I don't see why you took *me* along at all on this cruise. Second honeymoon, indeed!"

"And just *how* did I act with her? I danced with her, twice. Twice in a whole evening. Dammit, Ida, I'm getting sick of your acting this way. And beside—" Mr. Evans took a deep breath to go on, and thereby lost his chance.

"Treat me like dirt. When we get back—"

"All right, *all right*. If that's the way you feel about it, why wait till we get back? If you think *I'm* enjoying—"

Somehow that silence of only a fraction of a second on the radio stopped him. "And now a word from our sponsor . . ."

And half a minute later, with the radio again playing Strauss, Wade Evans was still staring at it in utter bewilderment. Finally he said, "What was *that?*"

Ida Evans looked at him wide-eyed. "You know, I had the funniest feeling that that was talking to us, to *me?* Like it was telling us to g-go ahead and fight, like we were starting to."

Mr. Evans laughed a little uncertainly. "Me, too. Like it *told* us to. And the funny thing is, now I don't want to." He walked over and turned the radio off. "Listen, Ida, do we *have* to fight? After all, this *is* our second honeymoon. Why not—listen, Ida, do you really want to go night-clubbing this evening?"

"Well—I do want to see Singapore, a little, and this is our only night here, but—it's early; we don't have to go out right away."

I don't mean of course, that everybody who heard that radio announcement was fighting, physically or verbally, or even thinking about fighting. And of course there were a couple of billion people who didn't hear it at all because they either didn't have radio sets or didn't happen to have them turned on. But almost everybody heard *about* it. Maybe not all of the African pygmies or all of the Australian bushmen, no, but every intelligent person in a civilized or semi-civilized country heard of it sooner or later and generally sooner.

And the point is, if there is a point, that those who *were* fighting or thinking of fighting and who happened to be within hearing distance of a turned-on radio . . .

Eight-thirty o'clock continued its way around the world. Mostly in jumps of an even hour from time-zone to time-zone, but not always; some time-zones vary for that system —as Singapore, on the half hour; as Calcutta, seven minutes short of the hour. But by regular or irregular intervals, the phenomenon of the word continued its way from east to west, happening everywhere at eight-thirty o'clock precisely.

Delhi, Teheran, Baghdad, Moscow. The Iron Curtain, in 1954, was stronger, more impenetrable than it had ever been before, so nothing was known at the time of the effect of the broadcast there; later it was learned that the course of events there was quite similar to the course of events in Washington, D. C., Berlin, Paris, London . . .

Washington. The President was in special conference with several members of the cabinet and the majority and minority leaders of the Senate. The Secretary of Defense was speaking, very quietly: "Gentlemen, I say again that our best, perhaps our only, chance of winning is to get there first. If we don't, they will. Everything shows that. Those confidential reports of yours, Mr. President, are absolute proof that they intend to attack. We *must*—"

A discreet tap on the door caused him to stop in midsentence.

The President said, "That's Walter—about the broadcast," and then louder, "Come in."

The President's confidential secretary came in. "Everything is ready, Mr. President," he said. "You said you wished to hear it yourself. These other gentlemen—?"

The President nodded, "We'll all go," he said. He stood, and then the others. "How many sets, Walter?"

"Six. We've tuned them to six different stations; two in this time belt, Washington and New York; two in other parts of this country, Denver and San Francisco; two foreign stations, Paris and Tokyo."

"Excellent," said the President. "Shall we go and hear this mysterious broadcast that all Europe and Asia are excited about?"

The Secretary of Defense smiled. "If you wish. But I doubt we'll hear anything. Getting control of the stations here—" He shrugged.

"Walter," said the President, "has there been anything further from Europe or Asia?"

"Nothing new, sir. Nothing has happened there since eight-thirty, their time. But confirmations of what did happen then are increasing. Everybody who was listening to any station at eight-thirty heard it. Whether the station was in their time zone or not. For instance, a radio set in

London which happened to be tuned to Athens, Greece, got the broadcast at eight-thirty, London—that is, Greenwich—time. Local sets in Athens tuned to the same station had heard it at eight-thirty Athens time—two hours earlier."

The majority leader of the Senate frowned. "That is patently impossible. It would indicate—"

"Exactly," said the President drily. "Gentlemen, shall we adjourn to the room where the receiving sets have been placed? It lacks five minutes of—eight-thirty."

They went down the hall to a room hideous with the sound of six receiving sets tuned to six different programs. Three minutes, two minutes, one—

Sudden silence for a fraction of a second. From six sets simultaneously the impersonal voice, "And now a word from our sponsor." The commanding voice gave the one-word command.

Then, again, the six radio sets blared forth their six different programs. No one tried to speak over that sound. They filed back into the conference chamber.

The President looked at the Secretary of Defense. "Well, Rawlins?"

The Secretary's face was white. "The only thing I can think of that would account for it—" He paused until the President prodded him with another "Well?"

"I'll grant it sounds incredible, but—a space-ship? Cruising around the world at the even rate of its period of revolution—a little over a thousand miles an hour. Over each point which it passes—which would be at the same hour everywhere—it momentarily blanks out other stations and puts on its own broadcast."

The Senate's majority leader snorted. "Why a space ship? There are planes that can travel that fast."

"Ever hear of radar? With our new installations along the coast anything going over up to a hundred miles high would show. And do you think Europe hasn't radar too?"

"And would they *tell* us if they spotted something?"

"England would. France would. And how about all our ships at sea that the thing has already passed over?"

"But a *space* ship!"

The President held up his hand. "Gentlemen. Let's not argue until we have the facts. Reports from many sources are even now coming in and being sifted and evaluated.

We've been getting ready for this for over fifteen hours now and—I'll see what's known already, if you'll pardon me."

He picked up the telephone at his end of the long conference table, spoke into it briefly and then listened for about two minutes before he said, "Thank you," and replaced the receiver.

Then he looked straight down the middle of the conference table as he spoke. "No radar station noticed anything out of the ordinary, not even a faint or blurred image." He hesitated. "The broadcast, gentlemen, was heard uniformly in all areas of the Eastern Time Zone which have daylight saving. It was uniformly *not* heard in areas which do not have daylight saving, where it is now seven-thirty P.M."

"Impossible," said the Secretary of Defense.

The President nodded slowly. "Exactly. Yet certain reports from borders of time zones in Europe led us to anticipate it, and it was checked carefully. Radio receivers were placed, in pairs, along the borders of certain zones. For example, a pair of receivers were placed at the city limits of Baltimore, one twelve inches within the city limits, the other twelve inches outside. Two feet apart. They were identical sets, identically tuned to the same station, operated from the same power source. One set received 'a word from our sponsor'; the other did not. The set-up is being maintained for another hour. But I do not doubt that—" He glanced at his wrist watch. "—forty-five minutes from now, when it will be eight-thirty o'clock in the non-daylight-saving zones, the situation will be reversed; the broadcast will be received by the set outside the daylight saving zone border and not by the similarly tuned set just inside."

He glanced around the table and his face was set and white. "Gentlemen, what is happening tonight all over the world is beyond science—our science, at any rate."

"It can't be," said the Secretary of Labor. "Damn it, Mr. President, there's got to be an explanation."

"Further experiments—much more delicate and decisive ones—are being arranged, especially for the non-daylight-saving areas of the Pacific Time Zone, where we still have four hours to arrange them. And the top scientists of California will be on the job." The President took out a handkerchief and wiped his forehead. "Until we have their reports and analyses, early tomorrow morning, shall we adjourn, gentlemen?"

The Defense Secretary frowned. "But, Mr. President, the purpose of our conference tonight was *not* to discuss this mysterious broadcast. Can we not get back to the original issue?"

"Do you really think that any major step should even be contemplated before we know what happened tonight— is happening tonight, I should say?"

"If we *don't* start the war, Mr. President, need I point out again who *will*? And the tremendous—practically decisive—advantage of taking the first step, gaining the offensive?"

"And obey the order in the broadcast?" growled the Secretary of Labor.

"Why not? Weren't we going to do just that anyway, because we had to?"

"Mr. Secretary," the President said slowly. "That order was not addressed to us specifically. That broadcast was heard—is being heard—all over the world, in all languages. But even if it was heard only here, and only in our own language, I would certainly hesitate to obey a command until I knew from whom that command came. Gentlemen, do you fully realize the implications of the fact that our top scientists, thus far at any rate, could not conceivably duplicate the conditions of that broadcast? That means either one of two things; that whoever produced the phenomenon is possessed of a science beyond ours, or that the phenomenon is of supernatural origin."

The Secretary of Commerce said softly, "My God."

The President looked at him. "Not unless your god is either Mars or Satan, Mr. Weatherby."

The hour of 8:30 P.M. had, several hours before, reached and passed the International Date Line. It was still 8:30 P.M. somewhere but not of June 9th, 1954. The mysterious broadcast was over.

It was dawn in Washington, D. C. The President, in his private office, was still interviewing, one after another, the long succession of experts who had been summoned—and brought by fast planes—to Washington for the purpose.

His face was haggard with weariness, his voice a trifle hoarse.

"Mr. Adams," he said to the current visitor, "you are, I am given to understand, the top expert on electronics—particularly as applied to radio—in this country. Can you offer any conceivable physical explanation of the method used by X?"

"X?"

"I should have explained; we are now using that designation for convenience to indicate the—uh—originator of the broadcast, whether singular or plural, human, extraterrestrial, or supernatural—either diabolical or divine."

"I see. Mr. President, it could not have been done with *our* knowledge of science. That is all I can say."

"And your conclusion?"

"I have none."

"Your *guess,* then."

The visitor hesitated. "My guess, Mr. President, outrageous as it seems, is that somewhere on Earth exists a cabal of scientists of whom we do not know, who have operated in secret and carried electronics a step—or several steps—beyond what is generally known."

"And their purpose?"

"I would say, again a guess, their purpose is to throw the world into war to enable them to take over and rule the world. Indubitably, they had other—and more deadly —devices for later use, after a war has weakened us."

"Then you do not believe war would be advisable?"

"My God, no, Mr. President!"

"Mr. Everett," said the President. "Your theory of a cabal of scientists corresponds with one I heard only a few minutes ago from a colleague of yours. Except for one thing. He believes that their purpose is evil—to precipitate war so they can take over. You believe, if I understand you correctly, that their purpose is benevolent."

"Exactly, sir. For one thing, if they're that good in electronics, they're probably that good in other fields. They wouldn't *need* to precipitate a war in order to take over. I think they are operating secretly to prevent war, to give mankind a chance to advance. But they know enough of human nature to know that men are pretty apt to do the opposite of what they are told. But that's psychology, which is not my field. I understand you are also interviewing some psychologists?"

"Yes," said the President, wearily.

"Then, if I understand you correctly, Mr. Corby," said the President, "you believe that the command to fight was designed to produce the opposite effect, whoever gave it?"

"Certainly, sir. But I must admit that all of my colleagues do not agree with me. They make exceptions."

"Will you explain the exceptions?"

"The major one is the possibility that the broadcast was of extra-terrestrial origin. An extra-terrestrial might or might not know enough of human psychology to realize that the command in question is likely—if not certain—to have the opposite effect. A lesser possibility is that—if a group of Earth scientists, operating secretly, produced the broadcasts, they might have concentrated on the physical sciences as against the mental, and be ignorant of psychology to the extent that—well, they would defeat their purpose."

"Their purpose being to start war?"

"Not my opinion, Mr. President. Only a consideration. I think they are trying to *prevent* war."

"In which case the command was psychologically sound?"

"Yes. And that is *not* opinion solely. Mr. President, people have been awake all night organizing peace societies, not only here, but all over the world."

"*All* over?"

"Well—we don't know, of course, what is going on behind the Iron Curtain. And circumstances are different there. But in my opinion, a movement for peace will have arisen there, too, although it may not have been able to organize, as elsewhere."

"Suppose, Mr. Corby, your idea of a group of benevolent scientists—or ones who think they are benevolent scientists—are back of it. What then?"

"*What then?* We'd damn well *better* not start a war—or anybody else either. If they're that good in electronics, they've got other stuff. They'll like as not utterly destroy whatever country makes an aggressive move first!"

"And if their purpose is malevolent?"

"Are you joking, Mr. President? We'd be playing right into their hands to start a war. We wouldn't last ten days."

"Mr. Lykov, you are recommended to me as the top expert on the psychology of the Russian people under Communism. What is your opinion as to how they will react to what happened last night?"

"They're going to think it's a Capitalist plot. They're going to think *we* did it."

"What purpose could they conceivably think we had?"

"To trap them into starting a war. Of course they intended to start one anyway—it's just been a question of which of us started it first, now that, since their development of atomics, they've had time to stock-pile—but they probably think right now that for some reason we *want* them to make the first move. So they won't; at least not until they've waited a while."

"General Wilkinson," said the President, "I know it is early for you to have received many reports as yet from our espionage agents in Europe and Asia, but the few that you have received—indicate what?"

"That they're doing just what *we're* doing, sir. Sitting tight and wondering. There have been no troop movements, either toward borders or away from them."

"Thank you, General."

"Dr. Burke," said the President, "I have been informed that the Council of United Churches has been in session all night. From the fact that you look as tired as I feel, I judge that is correct."

The most famous minister in the United States nodded, smiling faintly.

"And is it your opinion—I mean the opinion of your council—that last night's occurrence was of supernatural origin?"

"Almost unanimously, Mr. President."

"Then let's ignore the minority opinion of your group and concentrate on what you almost unanimously believe. Is it that the—we may as well call it *miracle,* since we are discussing it on the assumption that it was of supernatural orgin—was of divine or diabolical origin? More simply, was it God or the devil?"

"There, Mr. President, we have an almost even split of opinion. Approximately half of us believe that Satan accomplished it somehow. The other half that God did. Shall I outline briefly the arguments of either faction?"

"Please."

"The Satan group. The fact that the command was an evil one. Against the argument that God is sufficiently more powerful than Satan to have prevented the manifestation, the Satan group countered quite legitimately that God—in his infinite wisdom—may have permitted it, knowing the effect is likely to be the reverse of what Satan intended."

"I see, Dr. Burke."

"And the opposing group. The fact that, because of the perversity of human nature, the ultimate effect of the command is going to be good rather than stupid. Against the Satan group's argument that God could not issue an evil command, even for a laudable purpose, the counter-argument is that man cannot understand God sufficiently to place any limitation whatever upon what He can or cannot, would or would not, do."

The President nodded. "And does either group advocate *obeying* the command?"

"Definitely not. To those who believe the command came from Satan, disobedience is automatic. Those who believe the command came from God aver that those who believe in Him are sufficiently intelligent and good to recognize the command as divine irony."

"And the Satan group, Doctor—do they believe the devil is not smart enough to know that his command may backfire?"

"Evil is always stupid, Mr. President."

"And your personal opinion, Dr. Burke? You have not said to which faction you belong."

The minister smiled. "I am one of the very small faction which does not accept that the phenomenon was of supernatural origin at all, either from God *or* the devil."

"Then whom do you believe X to be, Doctor?"

"My personal guess is that X is extra-terrestrial. Perhaps as near as Mars, perhaps as far as another Galaxy."

The President sighed and said, "No, Walter, I simply cannot take time out for lunch. If you'll bring me a sandwich here, I'll have to apologize to my next visitor or two for eating while I talk. And coffee, lots of coffee."

"Certainly, sir."

"Just a minute, Walter. The telegrams that have been coming in since eight-thirty last night—how many are there now?"

"Well over forty thousand, sir. We've been working at classifying them, but we're several thousand behind."

"And?"

The presidential secretary said, "From every class—ministers, truck drivers, crackpots, business leaders, everybody. Offering every theory possible—but pretty much only one conclusion. No matter who they think instigated that broadcast or why, they want to disobey its command. Yesterday, I would say that nine-tenths of our population was resigned to war; well over half thought we ought to start it first. Today—well, there's always a lunatic fringe; about one telegram out of four hundred thinks we should go to war. The others—well, I think that today a declaration of war would cause a revolution, Mr. President."

"Thank you, Walter."

The secretary turned at the doorway. "A report from the army recruiting corps—enlistments thus far today have been fifteen—throughout the entire country. An average day for the past month, up to noon, was about eight thousand. I'll send in your sandwich, sir."

"Professor Winslow, I hope you will pardon my eating this sandwich while we talk. You are, I am told, professor of semantics at New York University, and the top man in your field?"

Professor Winslow smiled deprecatingly. "You would hardly expect me to agree to that, Mr. President. I presume you wish to ask questions about last night's—uh—broadcast?"

"Exactly. What are your conclusions?"

"The word 'fight' is hardly analyzable. Whether it was meant in fact or in reverse is a matter for the psychologists—and even they are having grave difficulty with it, until and unless they learn who gave that command."

The President nodded.

"But, Mr. President, the rest of the broadcast, the phrase in another voice that preceded the command. 'And now a word from our sponsor'—that is something which should give us something to work on, especially as we have studied it carefully in many languages, and worked out fully the connotation of every word."

"Your conclusion?"

"Only this; that it was carefully worded, designed, to conceal the identity of the broadcaster or broadcasters. Quite successfully. We can draw no worth while conclusions."

"Dr. Abrams, has any correlating phenomenon been noticed at your or any other observatory?"

"Nothing, Mr. President." The little man with the gray goatee smiled quietly. "The stars are all in their courses. Nothing observable is amiss with the universe. I fear I can give you no help—except my personal opinion."

"Which is?"

"That—regardless of the meaning, pro or con, of the command to fight—the opening phrase meant exactly what it said. That we are *sponsored*."

"By whom? God?"

"I am an agnostic, Mr. President. But I do not rule out the possibility that man isn't the highest *natural* being in the universe. It's quite large, you know. Perhaps we're an experiment conducted by someone—in another dimension, anywhere. Perhaps, generally speaking, we're allowed to go our way for the sake of the experiment. But we almost went too far, this time, toward destroying ourselves and ending the experiment. And he didn't want it ended. So—" He smiled gently. "—a word from our sponsor."

The President leaned forward across the desk, almost spilling his coffee. "But, if that is true, was the word *meant?*"

"I think that whether it was meant—in the sense in which you mean the word 'meant'—is irrelevant. If we have a sponsor, he must know what its effect will be, and that effect—whether it be war or peace—is what he wanted to achieve."

The President wiped his forehead with his handkerchief.

"How do you differentiate this—sponsor from the being most people call God?"

The little man hesitated. "I'm not sure I do. I told you I was an agnostic, not an atheist. However, I do not believe He sits on a cloud and has a long white beard."

"Mr. Baylor, I particularly wish to thank you for coming here. I am fully aware that you, as head of the Communist Party in the United States, are against everything I stand for. Yet I wish to ask you what the opinion of the Communists here is of the broadcast of yesterday evening."

"There is no matter of opinion. We *know* what it is."

"Of your own knowledge, Mr. Baylor, or because Moscow has spoken?"

"That is irrelevant. We are perfectly aware that the Capitalistic countries instigated that broadcast. And solely for the purpose of inciting *us* to start the war."

"And for what reason would we do that?"

"Because you have something new. Something in electronics that enabled you to accomplish what you accomplished last night and that is undoubtedly a decisive weapon. However, because of the opinion of the rest of the world, you do not dare to use it if you yourselves—as your warmongers have been demanding, as indeed you have been planning to do—start the war. You want us to start it and then, with world opinion on your side, you would be able to use your new weapon. However, we refuse to be propagandized."

"Thank you, Mr. Baylor. And may I ask you one question strictly off the record? Will you answer in the first person singular, not plural, your own personal, private opinion?"

"You may."

"Do you, personally, *really* believe we instigated that broadcast?"

"I—I do not know."

"The afternoon mail, Walter?"

"Well over a hundred thousand letters, Mr. President. We have been able to do only random sampling. They seem to be about the same as the telegrams. General Wickersham is anxious to see you, sir. He thinks you should issue a proclamation to the army. Army morale is in a terrible state, he says, and he thinks a word from you—"

The President smiled grimly. *"What* word, Walter? The only single word of importance I can think of has already been given—and hasn't done army morale any good at all. Tell General Wickersham to wait; maybe I'll be able to see him within a few days. Who's next on the list?"

"Professor Gresham of Harvard."

"His specialty?"

"Philosophy and metaphysics."

The President sighed. "Send him in."

"You actually mean, Professor, that you have no opinions at all? You won't even guess whether X is God, devil, extra-galactic superman, terrestrial scientist, Martian—?"

"What good would a guess do, Mr. President? I am certain of only one thing—and that is that *we will never know who or what X is.* Mortal or immortal, terrestrial or extra-galactic, microcosmic or macrocosmic, four dimensional or twelve, he is sufficiently more clever than we to keep us from discovering his identity. And it is obviously necessary to his plan that we do not know."

"Why?"

"It is obvious that he wants us to disobey that command, isn't it? And who ever heard of men obeying a command unless they knew—or thought they knew—*who gave it?* If anybody ever learns who gave that command, he can decide whether to obey it or not. *As long as he doesn't know, it's psychologically almost impossible for him to obey it.*"

The President nodded slowly. "I see what you mean. Men either obey or disobey commands—even commands they think come from God—according to their own will. But how *can* they obey an order, and still be men, when they don't know for sure where the order came from?"

He laughed. "And even the Commies don't know for sure whether we Capitalists did it or not. And as long as they're not sure—"

"Did we?"

The President said, "I'm beginning to wonder. Even though I know we didn't, it doesn't seem more unlikely than anything else." He tilted back in his chair and stared at the ceiling. After a while he said softly, "Anyway, I don't think there's going to be a war. Either side would be mad to start it."

There wasn't a war.

RUSTLE
OF WINGS

POKER WASN'T EXACTLY a religion with Gramp, but it was about the nearest thing he had to a religion for the first 50 or so years of his life. That's about how old he was when I went to live with him and Gram. That was a long time ago, in a little Ohio town. I can date it pretty well, because it was just after President McKinley was assassinated. I don't mean there was any connection between McKinley's assassination and my going to live with Gram and Gramp; it just happened about the same time. I was about ten.

Gram was a good woman and a Methodist and never touched a card, except occasionally to put away a deck that Gramp had left lying somewhere, and then she'd handle it gingerly, almost as though it might explode. But she'd given up, years before, trying to reform Gramp out of his heathen ways; given up trying *seriously,* I mean. She hadn't given up nagging him about it.

If she had, Gramp would have missed the nagging, I guess; he was so used to it by then. I was too young, then, to realize what an odd couple they made—the village atheist and the president of the Methodist missionary society. To me, then, they were just Gramp and Gram, and there wasn't anything strange about their loving and living together despite their differences.

Maybe it wasn't so strange after all. I mean, Gramp was a good man underneath the crust of his cynicism. He was one of the kindest men I ever knew, and one of the most generous. He got cantankerous only when it came to superstition or religion—he refused ever to distinguish between the two—and when it came to playing poker with his cronies, or, for that matter, when it came to playing poker with anyone, anywhere, any time.

He was a good player, too; he won a little more often than he lost. He used to figure that about a tenth of his income came from playing poker; the other nine-tenths came from the truck farm he ran, just at the edge of town. In a manner of speaking, though, you might say he came out even, because Gram insisted on tithing—giving one tenth of their income to the Methodist church and missions.

Maybe that fact helped Gram's conscience in the matter of living with Gramp; anyway, I remember that she was always madder when he lost than when he won. How she got around his being an atheist I don't know. Probably she never really believed him, even at his most dogmatic negative.

I'd been with them about three years; I must have been about thirteen at the time of the big change. That was still a long time ago, but I'll never forget the night the change started, the night I heard the rustle of leathery wings in the dining room. It was the night that the seed salesman ate with us, and later played poker with Gramp.

His name—I won't forget it—was Charley Bryce. He was a little man; I remember that he was just as tall as I was at the time, which wouldn't have been more than an inch or two over five feet. He wouldn't have weighed much over 100 pounds and he had short-cropped black hair that started rather low on his forehead but tapered off to a bald spot the size of a silver dollar farther back. I remember the bald spot well; I stood back of him for a while during the poker and recall thinking what a perfect fit that spot would be for one of the silver dollars—cartwheels, they were called—before him on the table. I don't remember his face at all.

I don't recall the conversation during dinner. In all probability it was largely about seeds, because the salesman hadn't yet completed taking Gramp's order. He'd called late in the afternoon; Gramp had been in town at the broker's with a load of truck, but Gram had expected him back any minute and had told the salesman to wait. But by the time Gramp and the wagon came back it was so late that Gram had asked the salesman to stay and eat with us, and he had accepted.

Gramp and Charley Bryce still sat at the table, I recall, while I helped Gram clear off the dishes, and Bryce had the order blank before him, finishing writing up Gramp's order.

It was after I'd carried the last load and came back to take care of the napkins that poker was mentioned for the first time; I don't know which of the men mentioned it first. But Gramp was telling animatedly of a hand he'd held the last time he'd played, a few nights before. The stranger—possibly I forgot to say that Charley Bryce *was* a stranger; we'd never met him before and he must have been shifted to a different territory because we never saw him again—was listening with smiling interest. No, I don't remember his face at all, but I remember that he smiled a lot.

I picked up the napkins and rings so Gram could take up the tablecloth from under them. And while she was folding the cloth I put three napkins—hers and Gramp's and mine—back into our respective napkin rings and put the salesman's napkin with the laundry. Gram had that expression on her face again, the tight-lipped disapproving look she wore whenever cards were being played or discussed.

And then Gramp asked, "Where are the cards, Ma?"

Gram sniffed. "Wherever you put them, William," she told him. So Gramp got the cards from the drawer in the sideboard where they were always kept, and got a big handful of silver out of his pocket and he and the stranger, Charley Bryce, started to play two-handed stud poker across a corner of the big square dining room table.

I was out in the kitchen then, for a while, helping Gram with the dishes, and when I came back most of the silver was in front of Bryce, and Gramp had gone into his wallet and there was a pile of dollar bills in front of him instead of the cartwheels. Dollar bills were big in those days, not the little skimpy ones we have now.

I stood there watching the game after I'd finished the dishes. I don't remember any of the hands they held; I remember that money seesawed back and forth, though, without anybody getting more than ten or twenty dollars ahead or behind. And I remember the stranger looking at the clock after a while and saying he wanted to catch the 10 o'clock train and would it be all right to deal off at half-past 9, and Gramp saying sure.

So they did, and at 9:30 it was Charley Bryce who was ahead. He counted off the money he himself had put into the game and there was a pile of silver cartwheels left, and he counted that, and I remember that he grinned. He said, "Thirteen dollars exactly. Thirteen pieces of silver."

"The devil," said Gramp; it was one of his favorite expressions.

And Gram sniffed. "Speak of the devil," she said, "and you hear the rustle of his wings."

Charley Bryce laughed softly. He'd picked up the deck of cards again, and he riffled them softly, as softly as he had laughed, and asked, "Like this?"

That was when I started to get scared.

Gram just sniffed again, though. She said, "Yes, like that. And if you gentlemen will excuse me— And you, Johnny, you better not stay up much longer."

She went upstairs.

The salesman chuckled and riffled the cards again. Louder, this time. I don't know whether it was the rustling sound they made or the thirteen pieces of silver, exactly, or what, but I was scared. I wasn't standing behind the salesman any more; I'd walked around the table. He saw my face and grinned at me. He said, "Son, you look like you believe in the devil, and think I'm him. Do you?"

I said "No, sir," but I must not have said it very convincingly. Gramp laughed out loud, and he wasn't a man that laughed out loud very often.

Gramp said, "I'm surprised at you, Johnny. Darned if you don't sound like you *do* believe it!" And he was off laughing again.

Charley Bryce looked at Gramp. There was a twinkle in his eye. He asked, "Don't you believe it?"

Gramp quit laughing. He said, "Cut it out, Charley. Giving the boy silly ideas." He looked around to be sure Gram had left. "I don't want him to grow up superstitious."

"Everybody's superstitious, more or less," Charley Bryce said.

Gramp shook his head. "Not me."

Bryce said, "You don't think you are, but if it came to a showdown, I'd bet you are."

Gramp frowned. "You'd bet what, and how?"

The salesman riffled the deck of cards once more and then put them down. He picked up the stack of cartwheels and counted them again. He said, "I'll bet thirteen dollars to your one dollar. Thirteen pieces of silver says you'd be afraid to prove you don't believe in the devil."

Gramp had put away his folding money but he took his wallet out again and took a dollar bill out of it. He put the bill on the table between them. He said, "Charley Bryce, you're covered."

Charley Bryce put the pile of silver dollars beside it, and took a fountain pen out of his pocket, the one Gramp had signed the seed order with. I remember the pen because it was one of the first fountain pens I'd ever seen and I'd been interested in it.

Charley Bryce handed Gramp the fountain pen and took a clean seed order blank out of his pocket and put it on the table in front of Gramp, the unprinted side up.

He said, "You write 'For thirteen dollars I sell my soul,' and then sign it."

Gramp laughed and picked up the fountain pen. He started to write, fast, and then his hand moved slower and slower and he stopped; I couldn't see how far he'd written.

He looked across the table at Charley Bryce. He said, "What if—?" Then he looked down at the paper a while more and then at the money in the middle of the table; the fourteen dollars, one paper and thirteen silver.

Then he grinned, but it was a kind of sick grin.

He said, "Take the bet, Charley. You win, I guess."

That was all there was to it. The salesman chuckled and picked up the money, and Gramp walked with him to the railroad station.

But Gramp wasn't ever exactly the same after that. Oh, he kept on playing poker; he never did change about that. Not even after he started going to church with Gram every Sunday regularly, and even after he finally let them make him a vestryman he kept on playing cards, and Gram kept on nagging him about it. He taught me how to play, too, in spite of Gram.

We never saw Charley Bryce again; he must have been transferred to a different route or changed jobs. And it wasn't until the day of Gramp's funeral in 1913 that I learned that Gram had heard the conversation and the bet that night; she'd been straightening things in the linen closet in the hall and hadn't gone upstairs yet. She told me on the way home from the funeral, ten years later.

I asked her, I remember, whether she would have come in and stopped Gramp if he'd been going to sign, and she smiled. She said, "He wouldn't have, Johnny. And it wouldn't have mattered if he had. If there really is a devil, God wouldn't let him wander around tempting people like that, in disguise."

"Would you have signed, Gram?" I asked her.

"Thirteen dollars for writing something silly on a piece of paper, Johnny? Of course I would. Wouldn't you?"

I said, "I don't know." And it's been a long time since then, but I still don't.

IMAGINE

IMAGINE ghosts, gods and devils.

Imagine hells and heavens, cities floating in the sky and cities sunken in the sea.

Unicorns and centaurs. Witches, warlocks, jinns and banshees.

Angels and harpies. Charms and incantations. Elementals, familiars, demons.

Easy to imagine, all of those things: mankind has been imagining them for thousands of years.

Imagine spaceships and the future.

Easy to imagine; the future is really coming and there'll be spaceships in it.

Is there then anything that's *hard* to imagine?

Of course there is.

Imagine a piece of matter and yourself inside it, yourself aware, thinking and therefore knowing you exist, able to move that piece of matter that you're in, to make it sleep or wake, make love or walk uphill.

Imagine a universe—infinite or not, as you wish to picture it—with a billion, billion, billion suns in it.

Imagine a blob of mud whirling madly around one of those suns.

Imagine yourself standing on that blob of mud, whirling with it, whirling through time and space to an unknown destination.

Imagine!